ELIJAH STEELE

NWB

For permission requests, write to the publisher, addressed "Attention: Permissions Coordinator," 205 N. Michigan Avenue, Suite #810, Chicago, IL 60601. 13th & Joan books may be purchased for educational, business or sales promotional use. For information, please email the Sales Department at sales@13thandjoan.com.

Printed in the U. S. A.
First Printing, July 2021.
Library of Congress Cataloging-in-Publication Data has been applied for.
ISBN: 978-1-953156-34-1

CONTENTS

DEDICATION

To the Most High, God.
To my mother and sister, Annette Sims and Carlet Cavalier.
To Carl Cavalier, thank you for being my number one fan
and always believing in me through it all.

ACKNOWLEDGEMENTS

Mekhi Cavalier

Carlon Cavalier

Malik Cavalier

Danica Cavalier

Carl Cavalier

Stephen Capler

CTD Solution LLC

Victor Sims

13th & Joan Publishing House

Mr. Charles & Delica Downing

Mr. Omar & Melissa Docher

Mr. Harold & Cheryl Carpenter

Mrs. Theresa Smith

EPIGRAPH

LIBERTY NOR FREEDOM CAN EXIST IN THE ABSENCE OF EQUALITY.

-ELIJAH STEELE-

INTRO

TO KILL A MOCKINGBIRD

"TO CHANGE OURSELVES EFFECTIVELY, WE FIRST HAD TO CHANGE OUR PERCEPTIONS."

Daring to change the way that we perceive the world around us and the people in it is no easy feat. And in many cases, people are who they have endeavored to be as a result of their rearing, life experiences and the occurrences that served to shape their perspective. Even so, people, rooted in their ways, have the power to change if we dare to change the systems that govern the people.

This book and the creation thereof was a necessity to spark a greater discussion about the way that we police ourselves and our communities in the face of inexcusable injustice. It is my belief that we must never stop talking about the injustices that plague our country and our world and we must never cease to take action. These measures of systemic induced slavery by physical, mental and emotional bondage are real and worthy of our time and resources to eliminate the long lasting affects of inequity.

This story has been on my heart for many years and my goal in committing it to pages has been a labor of love, one that I hope you will open your heart to allow the greater message of grace and justice in. You can never truly understand a person until you have used their wings to fly.

CHAPTER ONE

IN REMEMBRANCE OF ME

A MAN'S FIRST ETHICAL OBLIGATION IS TO THINK FOR HIMSELF.

Before I went out to speak to the congregation filled with whites (young & old) and several of my peers, I walked into the restroom and closed the door. I stared into the mirror and smiled as I thought to myself, "if all goes well, this could be the biggest breakthrough for blacks and people of color in Louisiana since the abolishment of slavery. This would mean America could take one step closer to ending this race war, and no one race or class of people would have an advantage over the next because everyone would have an equal slice of the pie. Of course, there would still be issues and disagreements, but that's life." Then the negative thoughts seemed to hit me all at once and made me question myself.

"Why would these white people listen to your black ass?! Their lives aren't in any danger; it's you and your people who need saving!! Besides, you ain't Dr. King or Malcolm!!"

It was as if someone was standing beside me, yelling those words into my ear. Suddenly I felt small, and my once serious thoughts seemed quite naive as a young child whose imagination allowed him to see the world as this perfect happy place.

Before I could react, tears began to roll down my face, and the smile was gone. The last time I cried, I was sitting in my police truck before walking into Southern University's Auditorium for Alton Sterling's funeral. I wiped the tears away and thought to myself, "I have to give this a try. If these people would ban together with us, the outcome could be epic. For sure, the black leaders who came before me would be proud, shit they gave their lives for this. It won't be easy, especially during a time where police officers killed several black unarmed men and women. Not to mention the recent school shootings, church shootings, high racial tension, and the country being led by an incompetent social media happy president."

Despite it all, this was a step towards obtaining what seemed an unreachable goal of equality and justice for all who call Louisiana home, thanks to an unlikely alliance.

Deep in my thoughts, I began to think back to how I made it to this point in my life...

My first year at Jackson State University (JSU) in Jackson, Mississippi attributed greatly to my sense of pride as a Black man. Man, I loved JSU! Everything about that school screamed, "I am Black and I am proud!!" Don't get me wrong, I was always confident and loved being who I was, but JSU taught me even more, which caused the love and pride to grow. From the administrators to the students, everyone there seemed to be a part of my extended family.

I remember applying for financial aid in the financial aid office, when I met my mother who never gave birth to me. Her name was Mrs. Theresa Smith, but I called her Momma or Mrs. Smith. She was a short, light-skinned lady who was every aspect of the word beautiful. It was obvious she loved helping students by the way she spoke to each of us. She was always honest and spoke her mind, just as most Black mothers I knew had done. Needless to say, I never had to worry about being dropped from a class due to financial aid. I had other problems as a freshman. Like money for food, women, marijuana, and immaturity.

One day as I was lying across my bed, scrolling through my contacts inside my dorm room. I heard loud music and what sounded like a block party outside. I didn't go outside right away to see what was going on because I wasn't really interested. I was more concerned with trying to call one of my female friends to my room to chill while my roommate was gone. After about thirty minutes passed, I finally decided to go outside and see what all of the noise was about. It seemed as if the entire school had gathered in the middle of the campus for a party. There were different groups of females and males dressed alike with logos or insignias on their shirts. This was my first exposure to sororities and fraternities. The beautiful women of Alpha Kappa Alpha, Delta Sigma Theta, and Zeta Phi Beta were all "reppin'" their different organizations. The brothers of Omega Psi Phi, Kappa Alpha Psi, and Alpha Phi Alpha also represented while on the "plaza" of the campus.

The plaza was the main gathering spot for students and was filled with remnants of Black history. There was a brick paved pathway which ran from one end of the campus to the other. I was required to take an orientation class at JSU, which gave me a brief history of the plaza. I learned that in the 1970s, the now brick paved plaza was once an actual road called Lynch Street, which allowed traffic to drive through the middle of the campus. Even though the plaza had since been closed off and traffic was no longer allowed, signs of the '70s era still remained in the form of bullet holes. As freshman students, we were given the task of walking outside of the female dormitory and asked to pay close attention to the bullet holes left in the walls. I learned that several White officers had fired over 400 bullets into the building, killing two students and injuring 12 others. From that class alone, I was further interested in Black history.

I was exposed to prominent Black names like Medgar Evers, a civil rights activist who was assassinated by a White supremacist, and Emmett Till, who was a young Black teenager brutally murdered by Whites. To this day, Emmett Till's story lights a fire within me and pisses me off every time I hear it, but I love JSU for teaching me those parts of my history. JSU not only exposed me to some of the most intelligent Black men and women I have ever come into contact with, but it also forced me to choose a career path. I declared criminal justice as my major. When asked about my major, all I could think about was becoming a detective, dressing in nice clothes, helping the less fortunate, and solving crimes, but somewhere between the partying, women, and lack of studying, I began to struggle. By the early part of 2010, I knew times had really become bad. I was facing days where I didn't have food to eat. Noodles were my last resort when money was low. And since money was often low, I was forced to return back home to the West Bank of New Orleans and find a job.

Truthfully, I wasn't in a big hurry to get back to New Orleans. Even though I loved the culture, the spirit and uniqueness that came from the city, it always seemed to remind me of a less fortunate and uninformed me. I visited New Orleans at least once or twice a year during the five years I lived in Mississippi, but I hadn't lived there since 2005 when a lady named Katrina forced a large number of people living in that area of the state to relocate. Although she was completely tragic for others, Katrina was a blessing in disguise for me. In Mississippi, which is "the sipp" for short, I was exposed to a better school system where grades and test scores were among the highest. Despite the fact that the majority of the students were White, the Blacks that attended the school stood out by excelling in academics and sports. For me, racism wasn't a big problem in high school because the students got along with each other for the most part, no matter what their race was. Nevertheless, I was not naïve to the fact that racism most likely took place in a covert fashion instead of in a way that would be noticeable by the students. Through high school and college at JSU, I have met some people that I consider family. But my time in "the sipp" was up, and the only other place I knew to run back to was New Orleans.

God had to have been listening to the loud growls of my stomach and paying attention to my shortage of noodles. It wasn't long after I decided to move back home that I got a job offer as a correctional officer in Bigot, Louisiana, located outside of New Orleans. It wasn't exactly a move back home, but it was the break I needed. Besides, it was an early start to my journey of becoming a well-dressed detective. Even though prior to taking the job I had no idea the city of Bigot or anything surrounding it existed, I took the job. I didn't realize it until later, but it turned out to be a great career move. I now had an actual retirement account and my own medical and dental benefits, which may seem basic to a working adult, but it was a treasure to me. I could have counted on one hand the number of adults in my family who had a job with benefits that they could retire from. That's not a shot at my family, but I was definitely breaking a fucked-up cycle of being on the wrong side of the law or the wrong side of life, period.

Life was moving in a promising direction for me. I had a brown 2007 Pontiac Grand Prix, an apartment, and a steady income with a newfound hatred of noodles. Believe me, I didn't want to see another bag of noodles for a long time.

I began working twelve-hour shifts in the jail, which seemed to become a second home for me. For the first time I could say that I wasn't in the jailhouse to visit a family member; instead, I was there to further my career and to add to my bank account. I soon became accustomed to the loud sounds of the big steel prison doors slamming together and the inmates yelling back and forward to one another in the cell blocks. Besides serving the inmates their food and medication, or entering their cells to conduct head counts, I watched them from behind a glass pod that was for the on-duty correctional officer to sit inside and watch over the inmates. Inside the pod was a toilet, a sink, a computer, and a desk. I thought of it as a larger version of an inmate's cell. The glass was tinted so that the inmates could not see in.

Many days and nights I found myself staring at the many Black and brown faces inside the cells. Some of them were there for second and third terms. If I had not known any better, I would have assumed that they loved being caged like animals and having the little freedom that Blacks did have taken away from them. But the truth is that I did know better than that. They were unknowingly trapped in a vicious cycle of being misguided, mistreated, and taken advantage of. I understood what it was like being from the neighborhoods that they were from. I understood the mindset of a fatherless child or a man who came from a broken home. I was once that kid in the "hood" with only the neighborhood drug dealer as my role model. I also knew that the end result of living impoverished, uninformed, misguided, and closed-minded was usually death or jail. Most of all, I knew that the country in which we lived did not play fair and had not been playing fair for hundreds of years. For those reasons I felt pity for the conditions that my people were trapped in. However, I had less pity for those who committed rape or murder, because I believed that even the most misguided or uninformed man or woman understood the difference between right and wrong.

When the inmates were asleep, I often spent the night doing push-ups or watching videos on my phone. One night in particular, I came across a video series called *Hidden Colors*. It captivated my attention to the point that I forgot about what was going on around me. The video spoke about the culture of Blacks, the world in which we lived, religion, White supremacy, and what life was like for my ancestors before they were taken to America. I had to have watched those videos a thousand times over to be sure I didn't misinterpret anything. If you could have been a fly on the wall, you would have seen my eyes slightly squinted and a small portion of my face illuminated by the light on my cell phone. I already had my assumptions about this country and world in which we lived just based on my own experiences with life, but *Hidden Colors* revealed a great deal more.

There were times I reluctantly put the phone down to stand up and check on the inmates, who all appeared to be sleeping inside of their cells on most nights. One night in particular, Francis, a Black male inmate of average height and a somewhat slender build, was awake. He spent most of his time working out and reciting rap lyrics to himself in a mirror. He was usually allowed to sleep in a cell by himself because he always seemed to find a reason to fight his cellmate, but that day the facility was full. Inmate Jacobs, who'd arrived the day before, had the unlucky privilege of sharing a cell with Francis. And on this night, Francis wasn't rapping or working out. Instead, he was standing at the cell door with this pissed-off look on his face. He didn't push the intercom button or try to get my attention, he just stood there. I pushed the intercom button and calmly asked him to return to his cot. He didn't say anything, he just turned away and quietly returned to his bed, and I returned to my workspace and buried my face in my phone again.

When the morning came and my night shift was over, I went home and researched the Black men and women who had narrated the videos that I'd been watching. I also researched as much as I could about the information within the videos. Needless to say, I fell in love with my Blackness all over again. I was viewing life through a different lens now. I thought even if the information I was reading about was only half true, I'd rather be told a lie that would boost my self-esteem rather than being told that every great man in America was White. My newfound enlightenment inspired me to begin reading about two fearless brothers, Malcolm X and Marcus Garvey. They each had the ability to lead a flock of sheep to war against a herd of lions. Most importantly, they were both well-polished and able to guide our people from underneath the tarp of oppression and out of poverty. However, at the height of both of these brothers' fights against social and economic enslavement, the mental state of our people seemed insufficient, and the pressure from the powers that be was too great. No matter how new my high school books were or how great my high school education was, I was never taught Black history to this extent in which my quest to learn led me.

I returned to work the next night tired and worn out from staying up and watching videos instead of getting rest. It was my last night before the weekend, anyway. And on top of that, I had a security detail lined up to work at one of the local restaurants.

I pulled up to the front parking lot of the facility and saw Brian parking his new sports car (the third in the same year), two parking spaces away from me. Brian was a 35-year-old Black man whose wife was a doctor. So he really didn't have to work at the prison dealing with inmates every day, it appeared to be by choice. She basically spoiled him, if you ask me. "What's up, B?" I yelled as I shut my car door and walked toward him.

He yelled back, "Nothing much. You heard about Francis this morning?"

I thought, *Oh shit, I hope whatever it was didn't happen on my watch.* "No, what happened?" I asked as we met up on the sidewalk that led into the facility.

"Francis found out that Jacobs was in jail for molesting his own daughter. Francis waited until Jacobs fell asleep, and when he did, Francis choked him out. He punched Jacobs in his face so many times that Jacobs suffered a broken nose and broken jaw. But that wasn't the worst part. When the nurses checked Jacobs out, he was complaining of pain in his backside. The nurses pulled a plastic spork from his anal canal."

I shook my head with a slight grin on my face. "Man, you're lying." Brian was known to exaggerate.

But he didn't crack a smile. He pushed a button on his keys to lock his car as he looked at me and said, "No, man. I just saw the lieutenant at the gas station a few minutes ago. He told me what happened. Karma's a bitch."

"No doubt," I replied as I shook my head and began walking into the facility to get the night shift over with.

Although news of the incident was spreading, the night was going smoothly. The inmates were all in their cells and quiet. I didn't have to worry about Francis as he had been moved to the lockdown cell block, where he would be housed by himself. I believed he preferred that anyway. Even though Francis was gone and the other inmates weren't much of a problem, I stayed off my phone and paced up and down the floor much of the night. When the lights were off inside the pod, the screen from the computer illuminated the room. The darkness and almost complete silence became my time to think. And if I wasn't thinking, I was working out.

There were also times that I imagined myself as an inmate. It wasn't hard to do since I was closed in a pod for twelve hours at a time. The only difference was that I was allowed to go home after the twelve hours were up. If I stayed with that pattern of thinking for too long, I would do something to quickly change what I was thinking about to something positive or something that would benefit me. I'm very superstitious, and I believe that if you think about something long enough, whatever it is will manifest. I get that shit from my momma, she is the queen of superstition. My momma had me and my sister believing that when someone accidentally swept your foot with a broom, you had to spit on the broom or you would soon go to jail. I got older and thought, "*That's ridiculous!*" Even still today, my mom will spit on a broom with quickness. No matter if they were positive or negative, big or small, thoughts such as those helped me pass time in the pod, and before I knew it, the dayshift officer was coming through the door to relieve me.

On some days prior to leaving, I stopped by the motor pool to check out a police car for my security detail at night. The motor pool was a place where the Sheriff's Office kept all of their police cars and trucks. There was also a mechanic shop there to service the cars. I always felt that riding in a police car was more "my speed." It beat sitting inside of a pod looking at inmates all day. Since I was a correctional officer, I was only allowed to drive the patrol car from the motor pool to my apartment and from my apartment to the restaurant where I worked the security detail. Even though I was now two years into my career and had received as much training as an officer who was assigned a patrol car, I was still just a corrections officer.

I always made sure to choose the patrol car that was in the best shape. I even washed it and shined it up nice. I used so much tire shine that when the sun hit it, the tires would glow. I didn't plan on taking anyone to jail in it, but I still liked to look good. Besides, the restaurant was going to be filled with women after the nightclubs began to close around 2 am, and the afterparty always seemed to end up at one of the local restaurants when the clubs closed.

When I made it home, I always backed the patrol car into a parking space directly in front of my apartment door. I could have easily pulled forward into the parking spot, but since the car was so clean, I backed it in as if there was someone standing outside to admire it. My usual routine was to go inside, eat two grilled cheese sandwiches, take a shower, and go straight to bed. I had to report to the restaurant by 9 pm. I was cool with the manager, but I was sure to be there for 9 pm and no later because I needed all of my money. At the end of the night, the manager would pay me one hundred dollars in cash.

My uniform at night consisted of beige cargo pants, black boots, a tucked-in blue collar shirt, and my gun belt. I didn't carry much on my gun belt besides my gun, pepper spray, two sets of handcuffs, and a radio. When I arrived at the restaurant I always greeted the employees, especially the manager so he would know that I wasn't late. On most nights, there weren't many people seated at the dining tables. It was too late for the older crowd to be out, and the younger crowd was still in the clubs *turning up*. On most nights while on duty, I sat in a chair near the front entrance and used my phone for entertainment.

One night in particular, I began reading the latest news on the Trayvon Martin murder trial. Although it appeared to those watching to be an open and shut case, it was the biggest incident in rotation on the news. For many reasons, I knew that because it involved a young Black male, the case could easily end with the suspected killer walking free.

It had been my hope that justice would actually be served since the suspected killer was not an officer. This was the country's chance to prove to Black America that our lives did matter and quiet the storm that would surface if justice were denied.

I must have been reading different articles for a few hours because I didn't notice the cars pouring into the parking lot.

"Heeyy, Mr. Officer!!" a young White and intoxicated female yelled as she walked through the front doors accompanied by two of her friends who were holding her up.

I stood up and looked out the windows and saw several more cars filling the parking lot. *Let the fun begin,* I thought to myself. The crowd was always hyped, loud, and diverse due to all the clubs closing at once, and there were only so many restaurants open during the late hours. I had heard of big fights happening at the restaurant when the unruly crowds arrived, but I'd never actually witnessed one while I was working.

Well, not until this night.

To my surprise, by 4 am, the crowd of drunk men and women had come and gone. It was so slow that the manager paid me before I was scheduled to leave at 5 am. I took the hundred dollars and put it in my patrol car along with my gun belt. I kept my radio and my gun attached to the belt that held my pants up until it was time for me to go. After I walked back into the restaurant and sat down in my chair near the front door, three young White males walked in. They were all above average height, maybe six feet or more, and clearly intoxicated.

There was one whose name I'd soon learn was Barry. Barry was the loudest of the three and eager to entertain the other two by cussing at the restaurant employees. I stood up and told Barry that if he couldn't calm down he would have to leave.

"Fuck you, you can't tell me what to…"

Before he could finish his sentence, I grabbed his left arm and began walking him to the door. His friends soon followed. I pushed Barry outside and allowed his friends to walk out behind him.

As I began closing the door, Barry yelled out, "Who do you think you are, nigger?" He spit a piece of gum from his mouth into his hand and threw it toward me, hitting me in the chest with it. I quickly flung the door open and told Barry to put his hands behind his back before grabbing him by his wrists. From outward appearances and his actions, it could have been assumed that Barry was one of those spoiled privileged White kids who never had a real ass whipping because he refused to listen to what I was saying. Barry's friends had to have seen the ass whipping coming because they both backed away.

He managed to pull his left wrist free from my right hand and threw a punch at me. It seemed like he was moving in slow motion judging from the time it took him to throw the punch. I quickly dodged his fist and threw a right hook that landed directly on his left eye. He held his face and let it go again to get into a fighting stance with both of his fists raised. I momentarily forgot where I was or that I had a uniform on because I was now eager to beat the brakes off Barry. He yelled, "Come on, nigger!" and threw two more punches that missed me. I threw another right hook to Barry's left eye, which caused him to lunge forward, grab me, and pull me to the ground. I rolled over and got on top of Barry as I grabbed his wrist again.

"Stop resisting!" I yelled as I pinned both wrists close to his ears. Barry turned his head to the right and bit down on my finger and refused to let it go. I began punching him repeatedly with my right hand until he released me.

I stood up as the manager and another employee came out of the restaurant to hold Barry down until the other officers arrived. The manager stated that he'd called 911 and told them what happened. I could hear the loud sirens from the patrol cars before I saw the blue lights. Several police cars pulled into the parking lot, one after another. When they arrived, they handcuffed Barry, put him in the back of the police car, and began taking statements from everyone at the restaurant, including me.

After the medics cleaned and wrapped my finger, I drove home satisfied and grateful. I was grateful that I'd gotten paid and was not seriously hurt but satisfied knowing that I gave Barry the ass whipping he deserved.

When I was done showering, I lay across my bed, replaying the scene in my head. I had been in many fights before as a little kid all the way up through high school, but something bothered me about this particular fight; not to the point of losing sleep over it, but enough to establish a disturbed feeling. Then I thought about the look on Barry's face when he called me a nigger and asked me, "Who do you think you are?" He didn't intimidate me but his face was telling. He was shocked and angry. Shocked that a "nigger" stood up to him, and angry that a "nigger" didn't just let him have his way.

Up until that point, I hadn't seen racism displayed openly like that. Only in the movies had I ever heard a White person outright call a person of color a nigger. That may sound far fetched, seeing as how I am from the Deep South and lived in both Mississippi and Louisiana, but it's the truth. Most of the blatantly racist movies that I have seen were created prior to me being born, and a part of me believed that rhetoric was reserved for movies made in the past.

While staring up at the ceiling I thought, *this can't be the current disposition or mindset of people living in America.* I wondered if there were White people who still believed that Black people were to just sit back and take whatever they dish out. It was 2012, not 1960. Little did I know…

CHAPTER 2

FORWARD MARCH

NO MOMENT CAN SUBSTITUTE EXPERIENCE.

The next day, when 10 am rolled around, I had just fallen into a deep sleep, the type of sleep where if something or someone suddenly disturbed your rest, you would jump up confused and wondering what day it was. That's just what happened when my cell phone started ringing. Damn, I was late for work!! I jumped up and began making preparations, until I remembered that it was my off day. Before returning to my bed, I grabbed my cell phone off the dresser and saw that someone from the Sheriff's Office was calling.

I cleared my throat and said, "Hello?" trying to sound like I had already been up and moving.

"Sorry to bother you, Elijah, but the sheriff would like to speak with you this morning." Mrs. Ella, the sheriff's secretary, was a sweet old White lady who always spoke softly.

"Umm, yes, ma'am, I'll get dressed and come that way now," I said while huffing in the background.

I could only wonder what the sheriff wanted with me. Maybe Barry had contacted his attorney to file a bullshit lawsuit against me, or maybe it was regarding another case; only time would reveal. Once I arrived at the office, I saw Mrs. Ella sitting at her desk, glasses resting on the tip of her nose as they always did.

"Hi, Mrs. Ella."

She smiled as she whispered, "He's in the office, son" and pointed toward the sheriff's open office door.

"Come on in hea, son, and have a seat." The sheriff was an old, short, grouchy forgetful White man who loved to blow smoke up people's ass. On most days he would actually forget much of what he'd previously said, or at least he pretended to forget. He was a typical politician, if you asked me.

"I was told that you handled yourself well at that restaurant with that knucklehead. What was his problem? He didn't want to listen?"

"No, sir, he was cursing the employees, calling me a nigger, and he tried to hit me when I tried putting him into handcuffs."

He leaned forward in his big office chair and shouted, "Well, good, you should've whipped his ass!! How long have you been working in the jailhouse, son?"

"Just about two years, sir," I stated as I thought to myself, *Like you give a shit.*

"Right," he replied as he sat back in his chair, while he put his hand on his chin and looked down at the stack of papers on his desk.

I wasn't really sure where he was going with the conversation, so I began thinking about different businesses that were hiring. If he was going to fire me, I wanted to at least have my next gig lined up.

"How would you like to go on the road, son?"

"The road, sir?" I replied, waiting for him to explain.

"Yes, the road, working as a patrol officer."

I wanted to say *Hell yes!* but a simpler reply of, "Yes, sir, I would like that just fine," suited the moment better.

"Report to the motor pool on Monday to receive your uniforms, patrol car, and further assignments. I am also sending you to the upcoming patrol academy," he confirmed.

I refrained from the outward appearance of excitement, and instead remained calm. I wanted nothing more than to be promoted. And to know that I was being promoted after serving justice in the face of racism meant more to me than words could have expressed. I accepted his offer and left the office for the day, saying goodbye to Ms. Ella as I left. When I got into the parking lot, I allowed myself a quiet moment of celebration and spent the next few days mentally preparing for the academy.

I began acquiring new information from the moment I stepped foot in the building as a part of the academy. Even on the first day, I found myself sitting in the classroom learning about different laws and how they applied to various situations. I always thought back to the West Bank of New Orleans. Although I wasn't the worst kid walking the streets, according to these laws that I was learning, I had done my fair share of things that were frowned upon. I reminisced on the times when I was living life as a kid in the presence of drug dealers, murderers, thieves, and others who weren't considered "upstanding citizens." Out of nowhere, a law enforcement career found me, and there I was joining forces with the exact people I had always been taught to run from. I was now in the company of the people who were supposedly my enemy and those who I was taught were out to get me. The next few weeks were filled with learning and unlearning a great deal of information about the legal system for which I was now aligned. Most importantly, I learned why someone like me was necessary to law enforcement and furthermore why law enforcement was necessary to the world.

Although the program lasted almost two months, time seemed to fly by before I graduated from the academy. Having my momma and the rest of my family there to witness my graduation filled my heart with joy. The fact that she had only been home from prison for a few years made the moment that much sweeter. If she had never said one word to me about how proud she was of me, the look on her face told me everything I needed to know. After all of the pictures were taken and awards handed out, I remembered telling my momma to get in my police car. She asked, "Where do you want me to sit?" Even though I took the question lightly, I knew it was a serious question to her. Without saying anything, I smiled and walked around to open the front passenger door for her. For at least thirty minutes, I drove her around in my police car just to add to whatever proud feeling she was having as a mother. Oddly enough, she hated my driving. "Boy, you betta slow yo ass down in these people's cars," she said more than once. When she was quiet, I glanced over at her and saw her grinning. And in that moment, I knew that she was grateful for where we both were in our lives. I couldn't have asked for more.

The day came to a close, but my career and journey were just beginning.

THE NEXT CHAPTER

After the completion of the patrol academy, I was equipped with a deeper understanding of the law and the inner workings of the legal system. Now working at the Sheriff's Office, I was a quick study. And because we were always shorthanded, the workload was plentiful. We responded to complaint after complaint, sometimes without the necessary backup. There were domestic violence calls, shootings, drug dealings, rapes, and murders. As an officer I seemed to know everyone's dirtiest secrets around the parish. I began to look at things I saw in the news differently. The occurrences of shootings and murders took on new meaning. And the experience taught me to look beyond the surface and to identify some of the bullshit that the media was putting out to make the story exciting in a desperate attempt to get a reaction from the general public.

Now, two years into my new career at the Sheriff's Office, I began taking note of the all too common thread of systemic racism and a continuous theme of injustice. Why were unarmed Black men and women continuously being shot by White police officers? Was it just a coincidence or a series of bad luck mishaps in the Black community? I wanted to believe that the world was not so grim, but the evidence was unfolding to the contrary. As a law enforcement officer who had undoubtedly encountered "shoot or don't shoot" moments myself, I was also forced to bear witness to the instances of "nonchalant" responses by my White counterparts to unarmed Black men and women being gunned down in the streets. I was a witness to their empty actions in the face of injustice. At times I often wondered if it was truly hard to follow an officer's simple commands when in front of a gun. If the person on the other end of the gun would have just listened, was it possible they wouldn't have gotten shot? These were the types of discussions they had even in my presence as if it justified a means to an end. In my heart, I knew that running from an officer or not doing exactly what the officer has asked you to do in no way justified death.

As the months progressed in my role, I encountered a multitude of scenarios with both Black and White citizens that not only justified me pulling out my weapon, but also firing it knowing that the agency's policies and procedures would have protected me. I also began to learn that many laws were established to protect the officers, and not the people who we were trained to serve. We were taught to use our hands and items such as pepper spray, baton, and taser so we don't become reliant on drawing a gun when it isn't completely necessary. For some reason, we had some officers who were not only pulling their weapons but also firing these weapons and killing unarmed men and women of color. That was a major issue for me and for any other decent American who values all human life regardless of color.

Nevertheless, everyday shift work wasn't filled with someone being shot or threatening to shoot. The great thing about being an officer is you are exposed to new situations each day.

I remember beginning one shift parked on a dead end road underneath an oak tree with the bumper of my patrol car against a fence. I was catching up on typing my police reports, and I didn't want anyone sneaking up on me. I was assigned to the southern portion of the city of Bigot. The neighborhood I was parked in was usually where all of my complaints came from, so I thought I would stay close in case I received a call. I guess I spoke too soon.

The Sheriff's Office radio dispatchers began calling me over the car radio. "Headquarters to unit 177, copy for a medical emergency."

I thought, *Shit, here we go* as I grabbed the microphone and responded, "Unit 177 to headquarters, go ahead."

"Be en route to 1922 Centennial Drive, at the Centennial Apartments for a medical emergency," they said. "The complainant will be waiting near the swimming pool."

I was just one block away from that apartment complex. I placed my paperwork aside and drove to the apartment. When I arrived I noticed Bigot's volunteer fire department was on the scene. As I walked up, I noticed that the firemen were all standing around their firetruck and didn't seem to be in much of a hurry. I assumed the emergency wasn't much of an emergency anymore. Before I could ask what was going on, a young barefooted Black female yelled to me, "He's over here!!" She was standing near the pool area and pointing to the open gate which led to the inside of the pool area.

The look on her face told me to run, so I did. I ran toward the open gate and looked across the pool. I saw a crowd gathered around a small Black boy who was lying flat on his back, motionless. Everything around me became blurry, and the only thing I could see clearly was the little boy as I ran to him. The crowd opened up as I dropped to my knees and began administering CPR. His eyes and mouth were both halfway open. Everything about this situation spelled out that this kid had passed away.

Where the hell are the firemen? I began thinking to myself. *Their equipment could do more good than I am doing right now. Why the fuck were they just standing there?!* I continued giving chest compressions as I stared into his face for some sign of life. "Come on, lil man, breathe, lil man," I whispered as I continued chest compressions. Vomit began to run out of his mouth, so I stopped pushing on his chest and turned him over to his side. Finally the little kid let out a loud exhale as water began to run out of his mouth.

"You did it, man! You saved him!" someone yelled from the crowd. But the kid exhaled and never inhaled again. I placed him on his back again and continued CPR. Bigot's firemen finally walked up and just stood over me with their resuscitation equipment in hand. I moved aside and allowed them to work on the kid.

I sat on the ground next to them to catch my breath. My arms felt as if I had been in the gym working out all day, so I just sat there and stared as these White firemen moved in slow motion. It was as if that young boy's life didn't mean shit. Let's be clear, I did know some White officers that would have gone out of their way to save anyone's life no matter their race; they just were not present on that day. These White firemen were obviously raised differently or had a different agenda. I wanted very badly to tell them to either do their fucking jobs like that kid's life mattered to them or to get the fuck out of the way so I could do it, but that moment wasn't about me or my feelings.

As the moments passed, I listened to the family argue back and forth about who was supposed to be watching the kid. When I had finally heard enough, I jumped up and yelled, "It doesn't fucking matter!! Look at him! That shit doesn't matter!!"

Everyone stared but didn't say another word. I was relieved when the medics arrived at the scene and stated that the kid had a weak pulse and that they were flying him out to a nearby hospital.

Before leaving and going home for the day, I gathered information from the family in reference to the little boy being in the pool by himself. I forwarded the information to the detectives and went home for the day.

When I pulled up to my apartment my cell phone began ringing. It was the detective who was assigned to the case.

"Hello?"

The detective didn't hesitate as he stated, "Hey, Elijah, the kid didn't make it, man."

"What?! I thought he had a pulse."

"He had a weak pulse but crashed three times. Every time the medics would revive him, he would crash again. They just decided not to revive him anymore."

"Thanks for calling." I sat in my police car and thought about the little boy and how he must have felt trying to fight his way back up to the surface of the swimming pool.

No one was there to notice the little kid struggling or sinking back to the bottom of the pool when he couldn't fight to swim anymore. For some reason I felt as if I was responsible for him not getting a second chance. When he exhaled and vomited, I guess I witnessed him take his last breath. That was even worse for me. I wiped the tears away from my eyes before they could run down my face. If it had brought him back, I would have given every dollar I had to my name to pay for swimming lessons. That way he would have at least had a fighting chance.

The pain and sorrow I felt for the little boy and his situation was all too familiar to me. Those feelings dragged my thoughts back to when I was a kid and the first time my momma went to prison. She was only gone for a year, but it felt like forever. The lonely and deserted feeling that the kid had to feel at the bottom of that swimming pool was what I faced on a daily basis. My older sister and I lived with several different family members and tried our best to live a normal life with a smile on our faces. Despite our best attempts to be normal, we couldn't help but to notice the love and care our friends received from their parents.

When the school day was over, I would return back to whatever home I was staying at for the night, and I found myself crying without warning. There were times that even I didn't understand why I was crying. The thing I did understand, however, was that when I cried, no one was there to comfort me or assure me that everything was okay. Eventually, I was all cried out and came to the realization that I was my own comfort. The only difference between me and the little boy in the pool was that after I felt the pain of being lonely or being deserted, I was always blessed with another day to live and make my situation better. That little kid's opportunities had sunk to the bottom of the pool and would never be resurrected.

Once I got up to my apartment, I kicked my work boots off and left them outside the door. The smell of the kid's vomit was still fresh on the bottom of my boots. I must have stepped in it leaving the area of the incident.

Now physically and mentally exhausted, I sat on my sofa and stared at the reflection of myself through the glass of my television screen. I put my face inside of my hands and thought, *What a day*. My mind kept replaying flashbacks of the little kid vomiting as my phone rang again. It was my older cousin Derrick, who lived in New Orleans and was the middle son of my mom's oldest sister. He was the personification of "pro Black." Every conversation with him seemed to involve the government or the condition of our people. And in that moment, I honestly didn't feel like hearing that shit, but I answered the phone anyway.

"What's up?" I asked while placing the phone on speaker and setting it on my lap.

Derrick yelled, "Man, they let that bitch go!!"

"Let who go?" I asked as I grabbed the phone and placed it to my ear.

"Just watch the news, cuz. I'll talk to you later." Derrick hung up quickly.

I turned on the local news and saw a picture of Trayvon and read the words "NOT GUILTY!!"

When the news hit that Trayvon's suspected killer was found not guilty and would be set free, I thought, *Oh shit, Black people are about to band together*. A revolution was surely about to take place. The uprising from the verdict not only caused thousands of Black and Brown people to come together, but it was also the birth of the Black Lives Matter Movement (BLM). The Black Lives Matter Movement felt like the next best thing since the Black Panther Party. It made me proud as a Black man and a Black officer. Shit, I was just proud to be Black. I remember thinking, *If this is where the war between racist America and the people who are for equality begins, I will gladly shed this uniform and fight for equality.*

As the days and weeks passed, I was soon disappointed when I saw that protests quickly turned from meaningful to meaningless. News of rioting and looting was widespread. I knew the possibilities of how this would end for the protesters. All the police needed was a reason to start placing people into handcuffs and for the media to paint a horrible picture for the BLM movement. The headlines read, "BLM protest turns violent." Somehow I knew this wasn't the goal of BLM. I knew it wasn't the goal of the beautiful sisters who gave birth to this movement. I knew that everyone that was participating in the protests and riots didn't have the reputation of BLM in mind. A large number of protestors were there to get the attention of the government and powers that be, but others were there to just get attention. There wasn't any way to tell who was who because everyone had a BLM shirt on or was carrying a sign that read "Black Lives Matter." That quickly worked in the favor of the media and law enforcement. BLM was very powerful and grew very quickly. If the goal of the movement was to send a message to America that Black Lives Mattered, mission accomplished! The question was, how could we keep that message going as a community long after the protests were over? What things were we doing or not doing in our everyday lives to prove that our lives were important?

I turned the television off and just sat on my sofa in silence until my mind began to wander. I love my people, and I surely sympathize with our struggle that we have been battling for hundreds of years now. Without a doubt I would stop whatever I was doing and fight for my people, but why would I risk my life if we can't come together as a race to boycott a specific store or establishment? Some of us held that pride and dignity for ourselves, but everyone needed to be on board for us to rise up. Rioting and looting can't be the focus. Holding up picket signs can't be the focus. Just simply saying that you're "woke" can't be the focus. Participating in the "stop snitching" campaign when a Black person is killed by another Black person in the hood is counterproductive. Praising the dope dealer who sells dope to his own people is counterproductive.

Our actions always have to speak louder than our words. We have the energy needed to stand up to injustice as a race. We also have the resources and number of able bodies willing to fight alongside us. We just lack the consistency and motivation to stay true to the mission long after the "heated moment" is over.

I stared back at my reflection inside of my television and just shook my head. This uniform started to look less and less appealing to me. Not because of how I looked in it, but because of what the uniform stood for. Not what it was supposed to stand for but what the uniform meant to young Black America at that time. These unjustified shootings had all officers looking bad. I wasn't being paid enough to deal with the bullshit that came with being a Black officer. There was definitely not enough money in the world in which I could be paid to stand by and watch my brothers and sisters die in the streets like dogs. Was every shooting a bad shooting? No, but enough of them were bad in my eyes and apparently in the eyes of people all over the world. It was definitely time for a change.

I must have talked myself to sleep because I woke up on the sofa, still in full uniform. The clock on my cable box read 7:15 am. I got undressed and hopped in the shower just to put on gym clothes to go get sweaty again. I drove my police car to the gym, one of the places we're allowed to take our patrol cars when we're not working. Upon arrival, it was as I expected, not many cars in the parking lot. Besides the two pick-up trucks and another police car, it was empty. *That has to be Roger*, I thought to myself. Roger was a White guy who was about 38 years old. It was rare to not see Roger smiling or cracking jokes. He wasn't afraid to talk to anyone. Black, White, green, or purple, Roger would hold a conversation with anyone about anything at any given time. Roger was getting paid the big bucks. He worked for one of the top police agencies in the state. Everyone respected this agency, and their uniform was prestigious.

He had to have seen me coming through the parking lot because I wasn't fully through the gym door when he yelled, "What up, dude?!!" with his hands raised, smiling from ear to ear.

"What's up Roger, how's life?" I replied.

"Great, Elijah. I can't complain, dude. You know we're starting a new police academy in two months? I can put in a word for you if you're interested."

"Of course, if you don't think it's too late. Two months is just around the corner."

"You'll be fine. You're a pretty smart guy, and you're in good shape. Just go online, fill out the application, and submit it."

"I appreciate it, Roger."

I jumped on the treadmill and began with a light jog while I stared up at the television just above me. The media was all over the Trayvon story. "White cop kills Black man." "Family of Black man cries out for justice." With titles like these, a naïve person would be led to believe that the media actually gave a shit about Blacks and their grief. It was the same song and dance of a White news reporter going into a Black neighborhood to find the most inappropriate person to interview. I was convinced that this was a form of comedy for them.

I finished up with a light sprint to get my heart rate up and to get a good sweat going. Besides, I had to work the night shift later and needed to take my usual nap before then. Roger's offer to put a word in for me weighed heavily on my mind. His offer meant a huge increase in pay, a better retirement plan, and a chance to work in different areas of the state. I was all in. I couldn't wait to submit my application. If I got accepted to join this agency, it would be my biggest move yet.

When I returned home, I blended a bunch of fruit and vegetables to make a smoothie. And although I couldn't cook to save my soul, I made a mean grilled cheese sandwich to go along with the smoothie. After a quick meal and another shower, it was time for a nap. I lay down on my super soft pillow top mattress, which was covered by red silk sheets, and began to fall asleep. Until Cousin Derrick, who always seems to have perfect timing, decided to call.

Trying to sound like he wasn't interrupting me, I asked, "What up, cuz?! What happened to you last night? You seemed like you was in a rush to get off the phone."

"Damn, mister officer, you're real nosy. Lol, but I joined the New Orleans chapter of the Black Lives Matter Movement if you must know. We held a protest last night in the busy streets of downtown New Orleans."

"Oh yeah? How did that turn out?"

"It was amazing just to see how many people came out. Young, old, Black and White. There was a sense of unity as we all marched in the streets and chanted 'Justice or else!!'"

"Or else what?" I asked. "What happens after the protests are over and everyone goes back home to their business as usual? What was the goal of the protest and was the goal accomplished? Listen, Derrick, I am not saying that protests are pointless, but there has to be a goal in mind and a strategic way to reach that goal. Marching in the streets doesn't change any laws or cause a decline in revenue for anyone. 'No Justice, No Peace' is just an empty threat if it's not followed up by action."

"Well, maybe you're right about some things, Mr. Officer. Maybe we can use a little guidance and a solid plan. Maybe we aren't seeing any immediate change from protesting, but you know what we do see and feel? Dignity!! Unity!! Most importantly a sense of pride, knowing that we aren't just sitting around not doing shit, Mr. Officer!! I can't say the same for you, man. You're just sitting back judging us. If you know so damn much, how about you take that uniform off and show us the way?"

There was a brief silence on the phone. I knew Derrick was upset because he was yelling the entire time.

"Nothing to say, Mr. Officer?! I didn't think so!"

Derrick hung the phone up before I could tell him bye or that he was right. Shit, Derrick was right. I didn't have anything to say because I have often questioned myself about how I could help resolve the current issues we're facing. How could I shed light on the issues as a Black officer? He hung up before I could explain that to him, and I was too drained to call him back. I hoped we could talk later when he calmed down, but at that time my nap was more important.

I slept for a few hours before my alarm clock woke me up. I sat on the edge of my bed to allow myself to fully wake up before going to brush my teeth and get dressed. I hated feeling rushed, but it was 3:45 pm and it took me at least an hour to iron my uniform, shine my boots, and get my bulletproof vest and gun belt to fit me in a comfortable way. We were required to report to the motor pool by 5 pm before shift began at 6 pm to be given our assigned areas for the night. I didn't live far from the motor pool, so I was always on time or five minutes early.

When I walked into the motor pool, I was greeted by a poster that had been on the wall since I'd started my career with the Sheriff's Department that read, "FBI's Most Wanted!" A picture of a Black woman was displayed at the top of it. I stopped in front of the poster to read it every time I entered the motor pool. It never seemed to get old to me. This woman was beautiful. She wore long locs and was smiling ear to ear in her photo. The gap between her teeth added character to her smile. When I first saw the poster, I must have stood in front of it for at least five minutes staring at her and reading up on the reason behind her being wanted by the law. According to the poster, she was charged with the murder of a New Jersey state trooper. While in police custody she'd managed to escape and flee the country. It went on to say that she was a terrorist and was a part of the "Black Liberation Army." Above her picture read: JOANNE DEBORAH CHESIMARD in bold red letters. There were various aliases listed, but one of the most beautiful names I have ever heard given to a woman was Assata Shakur. There was strength and beauty in the name

Assata Shakur. After doing research and learning her story, she'd piqued my interest and become sort of a hero to me. I definitely didn't see her as a terrorist. Standing in front of her poster and reading was my way of connecting with her, although I knew that it was likely that I would never meet her. The truth was that I secretly admired anyone that maintained a warrior's spirit in the face of injustice. And while under no circumstances did I condone death that was unjust, I did cling to the notice of justice for all.

CHAPTER THREE

MUTED MUTINY

A SHIP OF DEMOCRACY CAN NOT CONQUER THE OCEAN IF ITS SAILORS ARE YET OPPRESSED.

I was startled by a voice just behind me. "Hey, Steele! Are you ready to work or are you going to stand there and stare a hole in that poster?"

I replied, "Yeah, Lieutenant, I'm good."

Lieutenant Robert was my shift supervisor. He finally lifted his head up from the stack of reports he had been checking and noticed me staring at the poster again. Lieutenant Robert was a laid-back supervisor for the most part. He was a tall, heavy set, mid-age White guy. He'd been with the department for about ten years and had some family members working with the department as well. He was an ass kisser, so it wasn't a secret how he was promoted to lieutenant with the work ethic of a slug. If you have ever watched Damon and Keenen Wayans' show *In Living Color*, you're probably familiar with Paul Mooney's character Homie the Clown. Even though Lieutenant Robert wasn't an extremely old man, his hair was bald down the middle just as Homie's was.

"Steele, you'll be assigned to the Westside tonight. I'll be close to that area. If you need anything, give me a call."

I knew it, I thought to myself. Westside was the busiest and largest area to cover. Whoever worked in that area would usually work without any other officers close to assist them. To make it seem not so fucked up, Lieutenant Robert would usually say, "I'll be close if you need me." In translation, *I'll be at my house* (which was near the Westside) *watching television so don't bother me.* The good thing about not having other officers around, was that you didn't have to worry about parking beside one another and holding an irrelevant conversation. I was always cool with not wasting time. After receiving my assigned area, I left the motor pool in search of my first cup of coffee.

It was my hope that the night would be a slow one. I was more focused on going online to complete that application Roger asked me to finish than anything else. I parked behind a huge Baptist church which sat off the highway on a large piece of land in the heart of the Westside. I was an equal amount of distance from each of the problem neighborhoods just in case I received a call. While sitting, I began filling out the lengthy application with hopes of finishing before I received a call or an alert. It was 10 pm by the time I managed to complete the application without being disturbed, which was unheard of while working in this area. I sent Roger a text message letting him know that the application had been completed and submitted. My goal was to leave no stone unturned for the opportunity he presented.

After looking down and realizing that my coffee cup was empty, I also realized that it felt weird not receiving a call for anything that night. I began patrolling the nearby neighborhoods to stay awake. Forest Park was a primarily Black neighborhood. There were apartments toward the front of the neighborhood, houses in the middle, and more apartments towards the back. Asians and Hispanics resided in the front apartments. The poor class of Whites and Blacks lived among each other in the middle, and the back portion of the neighborhood and second set of apartments was where the highest crime occurred. Drugs, shootings, and constant loud parties kept older men and women from living in that area, which meant that it consisted mostly of residents ages 25-35. Clover Lane was the street to turn down in order to reach the apartments.

The usually active and crowded street of Clover Lane was nearly empty that night. There were a few dudes sitting on the back of cars that were parked in front of the apartments, but the neighborhood was quiet for the most part. I wasn't complaining at all. I was already tired of driving and ready to go back to my hideout behind the church. I stopped at a nearby fast food spot and took advantage of the dollar menu before arriving back at the church. This food, although only a dollar, gave me a clear understanding of why most officers die of heart disease rather than being shot. This is the only food available while working late nights, it tastes good, and it's cheap.

Just as I started to dig in, my phone began ringing. It was Derrick. I for sure didn't expect him to call me this soon. Maybe he felt like he overreacted and wanted to make peace just as much as I did.

"What's up, cuz? It's Derrick."

"Yeah, I know," I responded. "What's up with you, Derrick?"

"I'm okay, I can't complain."

I sensed that there was still tension between us, and the conversation would become uncomfortable if I didn't get what I had to say off of my chest. I slid down in my seat to get comfortable, took a deep breath, and said, "Look, cuz, I know shit got heated when we last spoke, but let me be the first to say I apologize and that you were right. Being a Black officer comes with a lot of baggage, man, and I am oftentimes conflicted. I want to be involved with the movements that will help liberate our people and other oppressed people, but I fear if I leave my current position to go all in, it'll be for nothing. Lose my career to participate in a riot? I'm supposed to risk it all for some halfway committed people? We're proclaiming justice or else, then a week later we're back to the no snitching campaign when someone from the hood gets shot by someone else from the same hood. If I was faced with these decisions when Malcolm or Martin was here, I wouldn't have to think twice.

"Believe it or not, Derrick, I am not just sitting back and judging. I am actually making a difference from my position as a Black officer. Maybe if

we taught our kids that it's okay to become police officers, more neighborhoods would be policed by Black officers who could relate to the people
within the neighborhoods. We are lacking the leadership that our people
desperately need, and I want to help, Derrick, but how serious and committed are we?"

He said, "Yeah, I hear you. I didn't call to argue with you, but if you hav-
en't realized, Martin and Malcolm aren't here. So if you really want to help,
here's your chance."

"What do you mean?" I asked.

"I accept your apology, cuz, but that's not why I called. We're planning
another protest for tomorrow, and we can really use some guidance."

I laughed and said jokingly, "Stop fucking with me, man. Who's going to
take orders from a police officer on how to effectively protest?"

"We will, man. I told my group about you. I told them that you're a good
dude, man, and you really wanted to see a change happen for our people.
Look, we're out of ideas, man. The police seem to always have the upper
hand in every situation, Elijah. You said you wanted to help—well, here's
your chance. Hypothetically, if you were leading a group of your peers to
protest for a great cause, how would you do it?"

"Hypothetically?" I asked.

"Yeah, Mr. Officer, hypothetically," Derrick responded.

"How many people would you say are in this hypothetical group?"

"Ughh, three hundred and thirty, give or take a few," Derrick said,
sounding unsure.

"How does the group of people feel about possibly being pepper sprayed,
tasered and/or arrested?"

"They completely understand the risks they're taking and are willing to
fight for justice in spite of it all. We just need to know that what we're doing will at some point have an impact. We need to see some type of change
taking place as a result of our sacrifices."

"Understood," I said. "Well, if I was to lead this hypothetical group, I would tell them to be in more than one place at a time."

"What?!" Derrick shouted.

"Hear me out, Derrick. Get on social media and gather as many people as you can. Go into the neighborhoods and recruit as many people as you can. Beef up the group as much as possible, but divide your original members from the new members by the assignments they receive. Have strict time schedules on each assignment and stress the importance of each assignment being carried out without failure. Give the miscellaneous assignments to the new members of the group. That way they won't be scared away by the thought of being arrested or caught. The miscellaneous assignments should cause a delay in the response time for the assigned law enforcement and cause them to have to handle different issues around the city simultaneously. This will spread officers out and allow you to carry out your primary objective. Your main objective should not begin or be carried out until all other objectives have taken place and not a second sooner."

Derrick laughed. "Wow, how long have you been thinking of shit like this?"

I smiled and said, "I've had some time to think about a lot of hypothetical situations."

After a brief silence, Derrick said, "Well, I love and appreciate you for this, cousin."

"I love you too, Derrick, but that's enough of that sentimental shit."

"Headquarters to unit 177, copy a complaint!" Before we could end the conversation, the dispatchers began calling me.

"Look, I have to go man. Good luck with your protest. One more thing, if you 'hypothetically' go to jail, please don't call me from the jail phone, okay?"

"Lol, all right, man." Derrick laughed before saying goodbye.

"Headquarters to unit 177?" The radio dispatcher didn't waste any time calling me again. This couldn't be good.

I grabbed the microphone and responded with haste, "Unit 177 to head-quarters, go ahead with the complaint."

"Be en route to 9355 Clover Lane in reference to a home invasion. The caller stated that one subject was shot and the suspects fled the scene."

"Roger that, headquarters. Have paramedics en route to that location as well."

It was 1 am, and I knew a quiet night was just too good to be true, especially on the Westside. Unfortunately, Lieutenant Robert would have to get off his ass and back me up on this one, so I tried calling him over the radio:

"Unit 177 to Lieutenant Robert!"

"Lieutenant Robert to unit 177," he responded quickly. "I got the call, I'll meet you there."

"Roger that, sir."

I arrived at Clover Lane and a crowd of about twenty people were all pointing to a dark alleyway, which led to a slightly opened apartment door and shouting, "He's in there on the floor. Please help him!"

I exited my police car with my gun in hand. Lieutenant Robert pulled up behind me. "Is anyone else in there?" I asked.

"No!" I got closer to the open apartment door and saw what appeared to be someone lying on the floor. All I could see was a black tennis shoe and a black pair of shorts on the person who was lying motionless. I pushed the door open with my right foot and saw the victim on the floor. He was a Black male with a bullet hole in the top of his head. His eyes were wide open just staring up at the ceiling. I looked closer and saw that his shirt was moving. He was still breathing, very slow and deep breaths. His chest would slowly rise and fall again with each attempted breath he took. The hole in his head spit out blood each time his chest rose and fell.

Lieutenant Robert nudged me and signaled for me to move forward into the home. I yelled, "Sheriff's Office, come out with your hands up!"

When I didn't receive a response, Lieutenant Robert and I stepped over the young man's body to search the rest of the apartment.

The apartment was clear. Lieutenant Robert went back out of the apartment and stood outside of the door. "Are you okay, Lieutenant?" I asked.

The look on his face said that he wasn't and he wanted to vomit. "Yeah I'm good. Just tape the scene off and wait for detectives to get here."

"What? Lieutenant, this guy is still breathing!"

He froze and stared at me.

"Where the fuck are the paramedics?! Unit 177 to headquarters, tell paramedics to step it up, this guy is still breathing but is losing blood!"

Before headquarters could respond, the paramedics were turning onto Clover Lane. I forced the crowd of people back to allow the paramedics to get to the victim. When additional officers arrived at the scene to help with crowd control, I went to the neighbor's apartment to speak with who I assumed to be the victim's girlfriend.

Noticeably shaken, she began to speak, "Weee…we were in the house watch…ing a movie when they knocked on the door and shot himmm!" She tried to explain to me what happened through hiccups and hysterical crying.

"I know you're upset right now," I said. "If you need a minute to calm down I can come back later."

She grabbed a tissue to wipe the snot from her nose as she took a couple deep breaths to gather herself.

"Listen," I went on, "more than anything right now your boyfriend needs you to pray for him. He was still breathing when paramedics drove up, so there is a chance he'll survive."

Her eyes lit up. "My baby was breathing?!"

"Yes, he was when the paramedics took him away. I don't know what's going to happen but just stay positive and be hopeful."

"Thank you, Jesus," she cried. "I know he's going to make it. He's a fighter."

"Would you like me to come back later?" I asked again.

"No, we were sitting in the living room watching a movie when somebody knocked on our door. My lil girl and I just sat on the sofa while my boyfriend got up to answer the door. When he asked who it was, somebody said 'pizza man.' We didn't order no pizza, so we thought it was one of his friends playing a joke on us. He couldn't see anything through the peephole because the alleyway was so dark. When he opened the door, two dudes forced their way into our house. They both were wearing Halloween masks and dressed in dark clothes. When the first guy forced his way in, he and my boyfriend began fighting over the gun he had in his hand. While they were fighting, he put the gun to the top of my boyfriend's head and shot him.

"When my boyfriend fell to the floor, me and my lil girl began screaming. They told both of us to 'shut the fuck up.' The second guy ran through the house, searching through our stuff while the first guy held me and my daughter at gunpoint. After they had everything they wanted, they both ran out of the door. I called the police, grabbed my daughter, and ran to my next-door neighbor's house."

I attempted to console her in the moment by saying, "You did what you were supposed to do by getting you and your daughter out of there and calling 911. Detectives will be here in a few minutes to speak with you. I appreciate you helping me out so far, and like I said before, just say a prayer for your boyfriend. I wish y'all the best of luck."

"Thank you, sir," she said while wiping her tears away.

I walked out the door and ran into Detective Grinds. "Detective Grinds, how are you, sir?" I asked as I smiled and shook his hand.

"Elijah Steele, long time no see."

Detective Grinds was a White guy who stood about 5'6" and was about 35 years old. He was a real cool guy and never seemed stressed about anything.

I asked, "I'm guessing this is your case?"

"Yup, what cha got?" asked Grinds.

"Boyfriend, girlfriend and their daughter are inside the apartment when they get a knock on the door from two suspects posing as pizza men. When the boyfriend opens the door, two men force their way in wearing Halloween masks. A struggle ensues over a gun, the boyfriend gets shot in the head, and the two suspects flee the scene after taking items from the house."

"Okay, I'll go and see what else I can dig up."

I yawned and said, "It's about that time for me. Y'all got it from here?"

"Yeah, go and get some rest, Steele."

Lieutenant Robert was standing next to his police unit, laughing and explaining to the other officers about how he and I had to enter the home. As always, he was most likely telling the story to make himself look like some type of hero, instead of telling the truth that he was a nervous wreck just thirty minutes ago. I'm sure he left out the part where he completely froze up. The young officers seemed to be loving it, so I got into my police car and left the scene before anyone could notice.

My apartment was only 20 minutes away from Clover Lane, but driving home at 5 am after a twelve-hour shift would turn a "skip and a hop" into a road trip.

AGITATOR

My deep thoughts were disturbed by a knock on the bathroom door. I whispered to myself, "How long have I been in here?" I looked down at my watch, and only ten minutes had passed. Reminiscing about my past made me lose track of time.

"Elijah! You all right in there, cuz?"

It was Derrick standing outside of the bathroom door. He was trying to whisper as he spoke to me through the door, but the nervousness in his voice caused him to get excited mid-sentence.

Derrick whispered, "The priest will be closing out his sermon soon.

He'll be introducing you to the congregation next. You need to hurry ya ass up, man, and why the hell are you talking to yourself?!"

I moved closer to the door so he could hear me over the loud noise coming from the congregation. I pushed my head against the door and whispered, "Alright, cuz, I'll be out there in a minute. I just need to get my head together. I'll be ready, don't worry."

Truth is, I was worried too. From the butterflies in my stomach to the millions of thoughts in my head, a little motivation or some sort of inspiration would really help carry me through this. Then, a quote from the great brother Malcolm X popped in my head:

"I'm for truth, no matter who tells it. I'm for justice, no matter who it's for or against."

Those words have always spoken volumes to me, and in this situation, it reminded me to speak the truth before the congregation. It didn't matter how much I assumed it might offend them or how much they would disagree with me. I was obligated to speak the truth and to speak openly from my heart. I closed the lid on the toilet and sat down. "Speak from the heart. Speak from the heart," I repeated to myself while staring at the bathroom floor.

Why was I here to begin with? What made me step out of my comfort zone and risk my career to be here? If anyone from this congregation recognized me as an officer, my career would be over for sure. So why was I here?

Stuck in a pattern of recollection, my mind jumped back to my days at the Sheriff's Office which was now in my rearview mirror. That offer from Roger was my new reality. Even though I was still located in Bigot, Louisiana, my duties evolved. There was no more patrolling the neighborhoods, no more jumping from complaint to complaint, and no more being underpaid for bullshit. Now I was dressed in uniforms considered by many as prestigious with the fancy hat to match. This agency had more love, support, and respect from the public than any other agency.

When something major took place in the state, 9 times out of 10 we were involved.

For major politicians visiting the state, natural disasters, and riots, I guess we were considered the first line of defense on a law enforcement level.

The week of July 5, 2016 placed the agency on the frontline in Baton Rouge, Louisiana for a much needed and completely necessary protest for the shooting of Alton Sterling. Sterling's death came two years after Eric Garner's, Mike Brown's, and Tamir Rice's deaths, all unarmed Black men killed by police. Between those times, Freddie Gray, another unarmed Black man, and Sandra Bland, an unarmed Black woman in police custody, also died. The Black communities all over the United States were burnt out and tired of the excuses given when a White officer unapologetically and unjustly took the life of a Black American.

"I feared for my life." "He moved in a threatening manner." "He appeared to have a weapon."

Those statements seemed to be copied and pasted to every shooting incident around the US. My experience as an officer allowed me to see and smell the bullshit in those statements. I also sensed the bullshit in the actions of the officers during these shootings. Even better, the public, who had no law enforcement experience, began to recognize the nonsense.

The very next day, Wednesday, July 6th, 2016 the world watched as Philando Castile was shot several times on a Facebook live stream while his girlfriend and her young daughter witnessed the terror. The senseless unarmed killings of Black people was an epidemic that was spreading all over the United States. Having live video footage of an officer killing someone made this epidemic seem like it was something new to the world; the unfortunate truth was that it wasn't. Justified or not, Black men and women had been killed by police officers before camera phones were available. Camera phones and social media now provided the world with instant access to what was going on everywhere in real time. I was thankful to God for these raw videos that exposed everything to the world. The videos shed light on the systemic racism that has haunted Black people throughout history. Hidden agendas were being uncovered in America in more ways than one.

My mind raced back to July 14, 2016, when I was at my home enjoying a day off. The phone rang, revealing a call from my supervisor. I stared at the phone debating whether or not I wanted to answer. When my supervisor called, he rarely had any positive shit to say. I picked it up anyway.

"What's up, man?" The frustration in my voice could have been easily translated into "Why the fuck are you calling me on my off day?"

"Hey, Steele! Look, man, sorry to bother you on your off day, but I was told by my supervisors to send you to Baton Rouge tomorrow for Alton Sterling's funeral."

I remembered thinking, *Why me?* There were plenty of others who had more time on the job. Furthermore, I had never just been given extra assignments without asking for them. Well, not any good assignments, I should say. I knew this was some bullshit, but if I declined I would have been written up for disobeying a direct order. I accepted the assignment and hung up the phone.

After the call, I sat in deep thought sifting through the potential reasons why I had been selected for an assignment such as this one. It wouldn't hit me until I met up with the other officers attending the funeral.

The next day, I arrived outside of Southern University's Auditorium, not as law enforcement, but as a human being with tears in my eyes. I pulled up behind several police trucks and just rested my head on the window. My drive there had been an hour and a half which forced me to bask in the notion of how fucked-up and unnecessary the shooting of Alton Sterling had been. I, like many other people in the country, had consumed many other videos documenting police killings around the country and was reminded how little my life and other Black lives were worth to racist America. Along with the upset Black people who were protesting in the streets, the videos showed the victim's family asking for peace and justice, which was never delivered. My tears weren't just because I was sad. Both history and present day proved indisputably that we have been robbed and stripped of our livelihoods. The reality that my people have been constantly getting kicked in the ass was not something that could be denied or ignored. Yet we were still the most forgiving in our pleas for peace and justice. At that moment, I felt pity for us, but here I was at a funeral, helping racist America clean up their dirty work. Even if I wanted to I couldn't stop the tears from falling, so I sat quietly in my police truck until the tears stopped.

The noise from the other officers shutting their doors caused me to lift my head and prepare to go into the building. I grabbed my clip-on tie and dried my eyes with it before putting it on. I followed the other officers, who were all Black and a bit older than me. They also seemed to know where they were going. I held my hat in my hand as we walked down a long hallway which led us to a large meeting room. When I entered the room, my eyes lit up. It was filled with officers from my agency and a few from the local agencies in Baton Rouge. I was taken aback by how many Black officers filled the room. I was not aware that the agency had that many Blacks, which was still minute compared to the number of Whites. We had them outnumbered on this day. But why? Another layer of the hidden agenda was obvious once we all received our assignments and began speaking to one another about the series of events taking place. If you have any experience in law enforcement, then you understand that when a bunch of officers get together they will begin gossiping like a bunch of women. To add to that, these men were Black and mostly mid-age or older men with much to say based on all that they had seen and done in their careers. The room quickly became noisy and filled with loud conversations. There were groups of officers huddled up in different areas of the room. A bystander might assume it was a large family reunion. Some of those men had been hired on to the department together but hadn't seen each other in years.

After I made my rounds, speaking to everyone and shaking hands, I went to the back of the room and sat next to an officer named Dennis. Dennis was a light skinned Black male who stood about 6'4". He was 42 years old but looked younger and could talk your ear off about anything. It wasn't hard to tell that any of us were from the South, but Dennis was from Alabama and had a very deep country accent. He wasn't scared to speak his mind, and he had no interest in speaking what most people call "proper English."

Dennis and a couple of other guys were already in deep conversation by the time I sat in the metal fold-up chair next to him. "Man, ain't nobody worried about these White folks, cuz!" Dennis shouted. "You have to be a dummy to think it's just a coincidence that over 90 percent of us here are Black. They done killed this man now they sending our Black asses to keep everything peaceful at the funeral!"

The sad part was that he was right, and we all knew it. This was a violation of the department's policy. The policy points out the fact that no one should be given an assignment based on race. This was one of many issues Blacks had with the department among others such as being disciplined for things that White officers weren't being disciplined for and being passed over for promotion by less qualified White officers.

Dennis was too deep into his conversation to notice I was next to him until I nudged him with my elbow.

"What's up, big brotha?"

He whipped his head to the right and smiled when he saw it was me. "What's up, man? I guess they got all of us here. God forbid something happens to us in this building. We won't have no Blacks left in our department," Dennis said jokingly.

We both smiled as we stood up and greeted one another with a quick handshake and a hug.

I caught a glimpse of the looks on the other guys' faces behind Dennis's back as he gave me a hug. They seemed relieved that I came over and interrupted his extended sermon. Even though these guys were Black, they were also against anything that could possibly ruin their careers. They were the type of guys who knew just as well as any of us that the circumstances weren't right or fair, but they would rather just let it be. I knew how they were before I sat down, and Dennis knew that they were cowards too, which is why he spoke freely. Dennis liked to be heard, no matter who was listening. He was well aware of the only five White officers in the noisy room who were sitting behind us, most likely listening to every word. I didn't mind that Dennis was speaking the truth to those spineless cowards. I would've spoken my piece as well, but I also recognized that we were at a funeral and this wasn't the time for it.

"It's about that time fellas!" Someone yelled from the front of the room. Everyone stood up and began to take their assigned posts.

We were all instructed not to engage the family members of Alton Sterling or any visitors. I walked out to my post which was just below the bleachers in the main portion of the auditorium. I was at the rear of the auditorium looking directly out at the stage area where the speaker would give his speech. Every news channel from around the state of Louisiana was there to cover the funeral. They were all piled behind the many seats reserved for the immediate family and friends. There was a curtain between myself and the news cameras which stretched from one end of the auditorium to the other. For some reason it was extremely important for the family not to see us posted up behind the congregation, and the curtain was supposed to hide us.

When the funeral began, visitors poured into the auditorium and filled the seats quickly. I watched through an opening in the curtain as the casket was wheeled into the auditorium and placed at the bottom of the stage. Two large photos of Alton were placed next to it. The photos seemed to expose Alton's personality. He had the biggest smile on his face that showed all of his gold teeth. I didn't know him personally, but if I had to guess I would have bet that he was a big teddy bear, someone who loved to joke and clown around. Someone his size could easily intimidate a coward or racist who had a badge and gun, not knowing that a simple conversation would reveal that he was harmless. It didn't go that way, so here Alton was, lying in his casket on display for the world to see.

Reverend Al Sharpton and Jesse Jackson were introduced as the guest speakers for the service. The two iconic civil rights activists were dapper as usual and noticeably accustomed to services such as this one. I stood directly in the opening of the curtain and watched Al Sharpton deliver his sermon without fumbling a word. He said:

Tomorrow morning I'm leading a march in New York. Two years ago, Sunday. They choked a man to death on video…selling loosie cigarettes in front of a store. Two years later, they shoot a man, selling CDs in front of a store. We've got to stop from going to a funeral to a funeral. America needs to deal when wrong is wrong and whoever does the wrong needs to pay the price for doing wrong!

The reverend went on to say that we needed to take better care of our money as a race. We needed to be conscious of who we spend our dollar with and we needed to boycott businesses who supported the unfair laws that are passed by Congress. Those were great points made by the reverend, but they were also cliché.

When Sharpton and Jackson were done with their sermons, I remember standing there feeling like "Where's the rest?" Was that it? I guess I had watched too many Malcolm X speeches where every word he spoke penetrated my soul like thunder.

Malcolm said:

I for one, as a Muslim, believe that the White man is intelligent enough if he was made to realize how Black people really feel and how fed up we really are. And without that old compromising sweet talk. Stop sweet talking him! Tell him how you feel! Tell him what kind of hell you been catchin' and let him know that if he is not ready to clean his house up. If he's not ready…to clean his house up…he shouldn't have a house…it should catch on fire…and burn down. –Malcolm X

Those words from Malcolm, if played to a congregation of people today could, without a doubt, motivate everyone in the room. It seemed to me that Sharpton's and Jackson's sermons were "sweet talk" with the standard "we shall overcome" sentiment. I also recognized that there is a time and a place for everything, so maybe the "sweet talk" was the time and place for Alton's homegoing. I have love and respect for what Sharpton and Jackson have done for our people, but I couldn't shake the feelings I felt. Maybe I was expecting too much from them in their old age. Maybe their age wasn't a factor and I had them all wrong.

Maybe I was just tired of hearing peaceful talk while my people were dying in the streets. How could it be that we continued to preach messages of non-violence amidst the dismal circumstances? I didn't want to see my people losing their lives behind bullshit, but if they're going to die, they should die for freedom instead of dying over the neighborhoods they lived in. They should die for the liberation of our people, instead of losing their lives for material shit, the fame or the money. Maybe that's just it. The cost of true freedom is too damn high, and no one is willing to die for it. No one is willing to give their life just so their great grandkids could enjoy the fruits of their labor. As a race and a community of people, it seemed we had wandered too far away from the path our ancestors cleared for us. It seemed as a race of people we have settled and become comfortable with injustice.

Maybe I needed to just keep my thoughts to myself, while tiptoeing through life, accepting whatever society was willing to give to me. Maybe I was just a young nigga with a badge who didn't know shit and who wasn't going to do shit to help his people besides run his mouth!

Yeah, maybe…

CHAPTER FOUR

PICKING THE GUN UP TO PUT THE GUN DOWN

THE MAN WILLING TO DIE FOR FREEDOM IS MORE POWERFUL THAN HE WHO LIVES AMONG THE UNJUST.

The morning after attending the funeral service for Alton Sterling, I drove to downtown New Orleans to meet with Derrick at a coffee shop. He called me almost immediately after the funeral was over to tell me he wanted to meet with me. After getting through the busy downtown traffic, I pulled up to a coffee shop to wait for him. It was around 10:15 am, and the sun was shining bright. I sat outside in the patio area to soak up some sun. I walked into the coffee shop, ordered a coffee, and sat on the hood in front of the car to enjoy the scenery. The sounds of the busy New Orleans streets were soothing in the moment. It felt great to blend in with the rest of the civilians. No uniform, no gun belt strapped to my waist, no watching my back, and best of all, no answering a shit load of random ass questions. I was told often that I looked too young to be an officer or that I looked like I was 16 years old. I guess those were compliments, but unless you knew me personally you would never know I was an officer. My normal attire outside of my uniform was a white dress shirt, a bowtie, dress slacks, and brown or black dress shoes, which suited me just fine.

By the time Derrick arrived, I was on my second cup of coffee. As he wheeled his black SUV up to the front of the coffee shop, I could see his white teeth through the windshield. He was smiling ear to ear. I laughed as I made my way to the entrance of the patio and greeted him with a hug.

Before I knew it, his front and rear passenger doors opened, and out came two males and a female whom I'd never seen before.

"Who are they, cuz?" I asked Derrick as his friends walked up to us.

Derrick saw the stale look on my face. He knew I didn't like surprises or hidden agendas. I could tell he knew exactly what I was thinking because of the fake smile he put on his face before introducing his friends.

"Elijah, this is Meisha, Kevin, and Joshua. Meisha and Kevin are both from New Orleans. Joshua was born and raised in Baton Rouge but lives here in New Orleans."

I quickly sized them all up. Meisha was medium built and dark complexed. She looked as if she was about my age, maybe 27 or 28. Her unprocessed natural hair was pulled back into a ponytail, and her Africa-shaped earrings matched the tone of her black halter top Malcolm X shirt. Kevin was a caramel complexed male who stood about 5'9", which was slightly taller than Meisha. He was wearing a black short-sleeved dashi-ki with gold trimming and black pants. His full but trimmed beard may have added a few years to his life, but I later learned that he was only 30. Joshua was a tall white guy, who stood about 6'3" with an appearance that would've suggested he was a hippie/revolutionary. His sandy blond hair was pulled back into a small ponytail which matched his rugged beard. He was also wearing a black Huey P. Newton shirt and black pants.

"Nice to meet y'all," I said with a forced smile on my face. "Might as well have a seat and enjoy this weather while we're here." I pointed to a table I'd secured before they arrived and moved aside to allow Meisha and everyone else to walk ahead of me. I thought to myself that Derrick was up to something.

After we all ordered a cup of coffee, Derrick finally began to reveal why he'd asked to meet with me.

"We all saw you at the funeral yesterday, Elijah. We were seated just above where you were standing."

I took a sip of my coffee and nodded my head. "Yeah, man, that was sad and very unfortunate for that family."

Derrick knew I was holding back what I really wanted to say because of the unexpected company. He continued, "Look, Elijah, I know you aren't completely open to discussing things like this in the presence of Kevin, Josh, and Meisha because you don't know them, and we get that, but we saw the pain on your face at the funeral. When we saw how upset you were, we came up with the idea of meeting with you."

Kevin, Meisha, and Josh all nodded in agreement.

"Well, I appreciate y'all coming to soak up this sun and enjoy this scenery with me. Like I said, it was an unfortunate situation." I continued to sip my coffee.

He continued, "That's not the main reason we're here. We're here because we want you to join us. We want you to lead our protests."

I sat back in my chair and casually glanced around to see if anyone else was looking before I leaned back in, looked him square in the eyes, and said, "I am a damn police officer, Derrick. Shit doesn't work like that, man! Are you trying to get me fired? It won't take long for this shit to get out that I am leading a protest or even having a conversation about leading a fucking protest."

Meisha, who had been sitting quietly the entire time, finally spoke up. "Who's going to rat you out? Elijah, look, I know you don't know us and your career is important to you, brotha, but it's obvious that your heart is with helping your people. We are doing everything we can out here, but we only know so much. The knowledge you gained in law enforcement combined with the knowledge you learned from the streets makes you a perfect candidate to lead us, bro, and we need you."

I heard Meisha's words, but I couldn't help being conflicted. What did become clear in the moment was how beautiful she was. From her pronounced, groomed eyebrows to her flawlessly defined lips which hid her bright-white teeth that gave way to her sweet yet strong voice, I was intrigued and inclined to listen to every word she spoke.

Kevin added, "You have already put trust in us without even knowing it, when you told Derrick how to lead a 'hypothetical protest.' We were on the frontlines of that protest, man. We knew where Derrick was receiving his information. No one ever spoke your name, my brotha. Has that information ever backfired on you in any way? Has anyone ever questioned you at all about helping us?"

I sat quiet. They were all right, and they all had valid points. A slight grin came across my face as I turned to Derrick and asked, "Exactly how did that protest turn out? I am aware of what was on the news channels, but how did it turn out?"

"I didn't think you were ever gonna ask," he replied. "Man, you don't know how long we've been waiting to share this with you. Where do I start, what do you want to know?"

Now fully immersed in the conversation, I replied, "Start from the beginning. I want to know everything!"

"Well, after I received the instructions from you, Meisha, Kevin, Joshua, and myself held mandatory meetings, one of which we held the same night. Of course we were the only three members out of the three hundred and thirty members who knew where this information came from. Everyone else in the group believed the three of us came up with the plans ourselves. We all met inside of an abandoned warehouse located in the Marigny District of New Orleans. We all went there from time to time to smoke our weed and chill."

Meisha stared at Derrick and cleared her throat. "The brotha is cool, but he's still an officer. Do you have to tell him about all of our illegal activities!?"

We all smiled as Derrick continued. "Anyway, like I was saying. We all met at the warehouse just before midnight. It was the first of three meetings, so about one hundred and fifty members showed up. The rundown warehouse didn't have electricity, so everyone brought a flashlight or used the light on their phones as we've done so many times before. The first night and the second night I spoke with the group about our plans and stressed to them how this protest was going to be slightly different from the ones we'd done in the past. Everyone was given the assignment to recruit as many trustworthy people as possible to be a part of the protest. I reminded everyone of the injustices we were facing and the recent unjustified police shootings that occurred at the time. Our mission was to get the attention of the local politicians and lawmakers. We wanted them to know that our lives mattered. We wanted them to know that if things didn't change, we held the power as a united people to force change. On the third night, we welcomed the newly recruited members. There were about fifty people who showed up ready to help. I gave out assignments just as you instructed me to. The new recruits were given the smaller tasks, and the detailed, more risky tasks were given to the original members. Everyone was split into different groups and was given specific times to execute their assignments. Once the assignments were executed, one group called the next group until the final call came to me. Let's just say your plan worked perfectly. Our message was received, and our voices were heard on that day. The local law enforcement was confused and unorganized to the point where the National Guard was called to assist. Some of us spent a few nights in the local lockup for our efforts, but we were awarded with even more followers of all races and backgrounds. Now with over four hundred members from all over Louisiana, we're stronger than we've ever been, and it's all thanks to you, Mr. Officer."

Derrick looked at me with a straight face. The same look Meisha, Kevin and Joshua stared me down with. I sat quiet again. They were clearly serious about me leading their movement. How big of a coward would I be to turn my back on my people knowing I could help affect real change? Even though my career was at stake, I would be just as useless as all the other great officers out there who remained quiet about injustices that plagued the country.

With both of my hands behind my head and all of my fingers interlocked,

I exhaled through my mouth all of the wind I had taken in through my nose. "Okay, I'll do it! I'm in, I'll do it!"

"Yesss!" Meisha shouted as she threw both her hands in the air.

"Shhhhh! Quiet, girl!" Kevin stated as he smiled from ear to ear. They were all smiling for what they considered to be great news.

"I'm in, but there are changes that need to be made. We need to be an organized group with values, standards, and principles that we live by. Our everyday lives outside of the group should reflect those same values and principles. No more accepting less when it comes to justice and the rights of our people. We will hold our own accountable just as much as we will hold others accountable for unfair treatment and the lack of equal opportunities. I would also like..." Before I could finish my thought, I felt a hand on my shoulder.

"What's going on, Mr. Elijah?" I turned my head just over my shoulder to see two local White officers whom I met a few times before while working in the French Quarter.

The mood in the air changed. "Hey, what's up, fellas?" I said with a slight grin, trying to pretend I was happy to see them. I wasn't. I was wondering how long they'd been standing behind me and hoped they would leave quickly. They were good policemen; it was just a bad time.

"We were sitting inside of the coffee shop when we noticed you sitting out here. Is that little Joshua?! Well, not so little anymore, but how's your dad and granddad?"

"They're both great, thanks for asking," Joshua said with a forced smile on his face.

"We'll let y'all get back to your coffee, besides we have to get back to work. Take it easy, Elijah!"

"Okay, fellas. Be safe and good seeing y'all."

I turned back around in my seat to all blank stares and Joshua's red cheeks as if he had just been embarrassed.

"Joshua, are you okay?" I asked.

"Yeah, I'm good. Those guys worked with my dad and granddad before both of them retired from the force after Katrina hit."

"Aight, you seemed a little flustered."

"Nah, I'm good."

"Okay, this brings me to my next thought. Let's be completely clear that we're not a hate group. We're not against all policemen just because they wear a uniform, just as we're not against a race of people because of the color of their skin. There are dirty unfit Black cops just as there are dirty unfit White cops. Now I am convinced that for every bad Black cop there are 20 bad White cops, but that's beside the point. The point is that we can't afford to give anyone a pass just because of the color of their skin or because they belong to a certain group."

"We get it, boss," Joshua said. "We are behind you one hundred percent. All we need to know is what's our next move?"

"We'll meet tomorrow night at the warehouse." Now thrust into an appointed position of leadership, I needed a moment to process it all. I said my goodbyes to Derrick, Meisha, and Joshua and sat for a while in silence.

Once I finally decided to leave the restaurant, I drove a few blocks, picked up a bit to eat, and headed home. That night, from my bed, I watched *Scarface*, which I'd seen a hundred times before. Once the movie ended, I turned to the local news channel and watched the news until my eyes closed and the television was watching me.

CHAPTER FIVE

SEEDS

IF REVOLUTION IS NOT IN YOUR SPIRIT, THEN IT CEASES TO EXIST.

The next morning I was awakened by the sounds of police sirens and loud talking. It was the news reporter and emergency vehicles on my television. The headlines read: **Baton Rouge Shooting: 3 Officers Dead.** I sat up in my bed and turned the volume up. From what I could understand, a suspect armed with a rifle opened fire on officers near a gas station. I found out later the shooter was a Black male by the name of Gavin Long from Missouri. Before traveling to Baton Rouge, Gavin expressed how disgusted he was with White police officers shooting unarmed Black men. He decided to skip protesting, holding up picket signs, or allowing the justice system to render some type of relief for the recent killings of Alton Sterling, Philando Castile, and others. He took things into his own hands and shot the first officers he came into contact with.

I got up out of my bed and began getting dressed for work. My mind stayed focused on the officer-involved shooting. Among the three officers who were murdered, one in particular stood out to me: Baton Rouge police officer Montrell Jackson. He stood out, not because he was a Black officer who was my age, but because of what he posted to Facebook just a week before he was murdered.

He wrote:

I'm tired physically and emotionally. Disappointed in some family, friends, and officers for some reckless comments, but hey what's in your heart is in your heart. I still love you all because hate takes too much energy, but I definitely won't be looking at you the same. Thank you to everyone who has reached out to me or my wife. It was needed and much appreciated. I swear to God I love this city, but I wonder if this city loves me. In uniform I get nasty hateful looks and out of uniform some consider me a threat. I've experienced so much in my short life and these last 3 days have tested me to the core. When people you know begin to question your integrity you realize they don't really know you at all. Look at my actions, they speak LOUD and CLEAR. Finally, I personally want to send prayers out to everyone directly affected by this tragedy. These are trying times. Please don't let hate infect your heart. This city MUST and WILL get better. I'm working in these streets, so any protesters, officers, friends, family, or whoever, if you see me and need a hug or want to say a prayer. I got you.

Montrell's message was heard throughout the US after the shooting took place. I felt his message in my heart and soul. He and I were fighting similar battles as Black officers, stuck in the middle of the battle between black and blue. We were amidst efforts to protect and serve everyone equally while in uniform while feeling the weight of oppression when the uniform was off. I believe Montrell and many other good officers suffered the consequences stemming from the actions and attitudes of corrupt officers and racist-oppressive citizens of America.

Gavin Long supposedly left behind a letter which some called a manifesto and others deemed a suicide note. Giving the letter a name wasn't nearly as important as trying to understand the clear message that was spelled out within it.

The note read:

PEACE FAMILY,

I know most of you who personally know me are in disbelief to hear from media reports that I am suspected of committing such horrendous acts of violence. You are thinking to yourself that this is completely out of character of the MAN you knew who was always positive, encouraging, & wore a smile wherever he was seen. Yes this does seem to be out of character but I ask that you finish reading before you make that decision.

I know I will be vilified by the media & police, unfortunately, I see my actions as a necessary evil that I do not wish to partake in, nor do I enjoy partaking in, but must partake in, in order to create substantial change within America's police forces and Judicial system.

Right now there is an unseen & concealed war within America's police force between Good cops & Bad cops. And the way the current system is set up, it protects all cops whether good or bad, right or wrong, instead of punishing bad cops & holding them accountable for their actions.

And when good cops do try and stand up, speak out, & point out the wrongs & criminal acts of bad cops they get reprimanded, harassed, black-balled or blacklisted or all of these and more. Thus creating a perpetual systematic fertile ground for bad cops to flourish, excel, & go unpunished in.

Therefore I must bring the same destruction that bad cops continue to inflict upon my people, upon bad cops as well as good cops in hopes that the good cops (which are the majority) will be able to stand together to enact justice and punishment against bad cops b/c right now the police force & current judicial system is not doing so.

Therefore now if the bad cops, law makers, & justice system leaders care about the welfare, families, & well-being of their fellow good cops, then they (bad cops) will quit committing criminal acts against melanated people & the people in general. If not, my people, & the people in general will continue to strike back against all cops until we see that bad cops are no longer protected & allowed to flourish. B/C until this happens, we the people cannot differentiate the good from the bad.

Protected & unpunished bad cops force melanated people to label the good cops as potential threats to the safety & well-being of our women, family, & children. Good cops, I ask that you help change this situation that we find ourselves in by starting from within the force & making an impact in there.

For the sake of preventing future loss of life rather it be from the hand of bad cops upon melanated people, or from the hand of the people upon good cops, I do not ask but order (With & By the power of the people behind me) for all bad cops to be punished swiftly, completely, & unhesitatingly; & for all unethical police practices & procedures to cease immediately.

Condolences to my people & their loved ones who have been victims at the hands of bad cops for decades. And condolences to the good cops & their families as well.

And special salute & thank you to the brave cops that have already identified & spoke up against bad cops and racist unjust practices.

After thanking several officers for speaking out against unfair treatment of Blacks, the note closed by saying:

"Sincerely, Love Cosmo

A sacrifice for my people, & a sacrifice for the people.

-LOOK UP, GET UP, & DON'T EVER GIVE UP!"

Long's way of thinking and the manner in which he carried out his form of justice was not the first time America had been exposed to it. In February of 2013, we were introduced to Christopher Dorner. Similar to Long, Dorner spent time in the military and fought for a country that would later play a part in his death. Both Long and Dorner were once considered "upstanding citizens" by America's standards. They were then, without hesitation, considered terrorists by public opinion and the media after choosing to take a stand against injustice and fight fire with fire. I believe we can all agree that the taking of one human life by another human is a horrendous act even if we have not completed the act of murder ourselves. Especially if that human being did nothing to deserve to have his/her life stripped away from them. Nevertheless, we can also agree that the history of America through slavery was built upon the fear-driving action of murder. America's argument for labeling persons like Dorner and Long as terrorists is that there are more peaceful ways to make one's voice heard rather than taking justice into their own hands and committing murder. America makes this argument with the dry residue of millions of innocent

Black slaves' blood on one of her hands and the fresh blood of today's mi-
norities on the other. I sympathize with the families who lost loved ones as
a result of the actions of Dorner and Long, but I am afraid that if we continue to just focus on Dorner's and Long's actions, we'll miss the fact that
the state that America's society is in causes a previously upstanding citizen
to become fed up and take justice into their own hands.

As long as America continues to ignore the cries and the mistreatment
of its people, the people will eventually stop crying. They will eventually
stop asking to be heard or to be treated better than second-class citizens.
The harsh reality of it, is there will be more Gavin Longs and Christopher
Dorners emerging from the loud cries of the people.

By the time I made it into the office to find out what area I would be
working in, the nasty details of the shootings began circulating in our
station in Bigot. No phones were ringing as they would usually do. That
meant there were no automobile accidents to investigate, which was rare.
The office was unusually quiet besides Dennis and three other officers all
standing in the front lobby. They were staring up at the television.

I can only imagine how this convo is going, I thought to myself. Dennis, a
loud-mouthed Black cop who held nothing back, speaking to three of our
boldest rednecks at the station and they were most likely discussing the
Baton Rouge shooting was a sight to behold. Kurt, Hebert, and Tim were
all assigned to the motorcycle division and were diehard confederate-flag
waving Trump supporters.

"What's up lil brotha!?" Dennis said as he greeted me with a dap and a
quick hug.

Tim, Kurt, and Hebert all turned away from the TV and greeted me
with a quick hand shake and a smile. "What's up, brother?"

Brother? I thought to myself. That word is used loosely throughout law
enforcement, but we were nowhere near brothers. Especially during a
time like this. The Trump era caused all closet racists to reveal themselves.
I mean if you wanted to really see these officers' true colors, all you had

to do was to check their social media pages, where they openly say things like "Mexicans should go back to wherever they came from."

That statement alone shows a bias. Coming from an officer, it's horrible. How could an officer aligned with such harsh sentiments treat a Mexican American with justice or tact?

"Y'all heard anything new about the shooting?" I asked.

"I think we got his ass," Kurt said with a smile. "They haven't said for sure, but I think we got him, bro."

Dennis was surprisingly quiet. He stood with one hand over his mouth and the other arm folded across his chest as he stared at the television.

My phone vibrated. *Let's meet at the warehouse tonight for 8pm.* Derrick sent out a group text with Meisha, Joshua, and Kevin included.

I wasn't excited about meeting at this warehouse. Shit, we could've just met at someone's house since the other members weren't coming. *We'll see how it goes,* I thought.

The lieutenant's office door was opened. He was sitting there staring at the computer with his glasses on the tip of his nose.

"Hey, Lieutenant, what area am I in today?" I asked.

"Morning, Steele. You'll be working Bigot today. Try not to make too much noise today, we have enough bullshit going on in Baton Rouge as it is. Stay close to your phone, we're all on-call for the next two weeks due to the number of protests we've been getting around the state."

Music to my ears. I'd just find a hiding spot and turn my police car into a movie theater.

CHAPTER SIX

INEVITABILITIES

IF PEACEFUL REVOLUTION IS NOT POSSIBLE, VIOLENT REVOLUTION WILL BE IMPOSSIBLE.

When I arrived at the warehouse for the protest strategy meeting, I thought to myself that the building was in worse shape than I imagined. It was one of the biggest buildings on the block. The graffiti on the walls, the tall weeds growing upwards and attached to the side of the building and the busted-out windows all led me to assume that it was still abandoned. At least I hoped it was. The last thing I needed was for the owner to show up tonight to find us in his building. From the looks of it, Derrick had found a way to supply the building with electricity.

I peeped through the broken window and saw a huge crowd of members all talking, laughing, and joking with one another. Kevin, Joshua, and Meisha were standing toward the front of the crowd. I couldn't see Derrick anywhere. Maybe he was among the hundred or more members running his mouth.

"Damn, this is a lot of people. This shit is really happening," I spoke quietly to myself.

"You scared, cuz?"

I turned quickly with my hand near my waist to acknowledge the voice speaking to me. It was Derrick with his hands in the air and a grin on his face. "Nigga, I almost shot yo ass."

I pushed my gun back down inside my waistline and hugged him.

"Are you ready or are you scared?" Derrick asked again.

"Nah, I ain't scared. I am nervous though. I'm not sure how the rest of the group will receive me."

"It aint like you're going in there to say *Hey, I am a fucking cop.* They still don't know who you are or what you do. For all they know, you're another new member. Go in there and speak your mind, cuz, like you do with me. If you want to tell them who you are then that's up to you. I have your back either way."

"You right. Let's do it."

Derrick threw his left arm around my neck and walked me inside. A few heads turned upon our entrance but immediately resumed their attention back to the conversations they were engaged in. Derrick and I moved through the crowd to the front where Meisha, Kevin, and Joshua were positioned.

"Welcome to the castle, boss man," Kevin said jokingly as he shook my hand.

I shook Joshua's hand before leaning in to give Meisha a hug. "Welcome, brotha," she said with a smile. I stared a second too long before refocusing.

As I turned to face the crowd, Derrick said, "Family, can I have your attention? Let's get started. We're welcoming a member to his first meeting. He's been a part of the family in a major way behind the scenes. Now we finally have him here. Welcome my cousin to the castle, Elijah Steele."

I stepped forward and looked around at the majority Black but incrementally diverse crowd as I waited for the light applause to stop. My stomach was in knots and my palms sweaty.

"Thanks, I appreciate the love," I said. "As Derrick said, I've been behind the scenes in the past. I didn't have plans of ever coming to any meetings, but here I am. I am here to help us become the most organized and well-trained group of protestors that exists. Every move we make has to have a reason behind it. We have to be as disciplined as the cops and other opposition we will be facing."

While I spoke, I glanced over the crowd to be sure I was reaching every-one. I noticed a dark skin brotha standing directly ahead of me out in the middle of the crowd. He was burning a hole in the side of my face with his eyes every time I looked away. He stood with an angry but confused look on his face as I continued to speak.

"Our goal should be to establish rules within our group. We should also have a set of morals and values in which…."

"You're the fucking cop who pulled me over!!" Everyone directed their attention to the center of the crowd from where the dark skin guy was yell-ing. He pointed his finger at me and yelled again, "You stopped me and my son! You're a fucking cop, nigga."

If I had ever wanted to disappear like Houdini, it was at this moment. But I didn't. I just stood there with a blank stare.

Someone yelled from the back, "The brotha just got here and you're ac-cusing him of being a cop. Let the man speak."

"He's a pig, and I know he's a pig because I saw him in full uniform."

A pig? My body quickly became hot. Now I wanted to kick his teeth down his throat!

Before I could say anything, Meisha stepped forward. "So what's your point? You're being rude to this brotha for what? Cause he's a police of-ficer? He's our police officer. We all agreed during our last meeting that our last protest was the most successful and organized, right? You even said yourself, brotha, that we needed to build off the greatness of the last protest. Well guess what, you're looking at the brotha who single handedly organized that protest!!"

The dark skin brotha stared and asked, "Is that true, Mr. Officer?"

I turned and looked at Derrick as he nodded in approval. "Yeah, that was me. The protest was my idea," I said as I stepped forward.

A voice yelled from the back of the crowd. "Hell yeah man, if we had more cops like you in our neighborhoods we'll be all right." The rest of the crowd agreed as they began applauding.

"Okay, so what? He's still an officer."

"What the hell is your point?" Meisha asked. "So what, the brother was doing his job and decided to pull you over. Did he arrest you? Just from knowing the brother, I'm willing to bet he didn't even give your ass a ticket, right?"

"Nah, he didn't," the dark skin brotha said as he shrugged his shoulders.

"Well, I'm willing to bet he smelled the marijuana in your car but decided not to search it. Here we have our ancestors being sprayed with fire hoses and being bit by police dogs for no reason. Then we have you complaining about being stopped by a Black officer who allowed your black ass to drive away totally unscathed. You're out of line, my brotha."

Meisha locked her arm around mine and asked, "Am I missing anything? Who else is against this brotha being a part of this family? Because if he's out then I'm out too!!"

"We all out!!" Kevin, Joshua, and Derrick said as they all stepped forward with me.

Everyone in the crowd seemed to agree with Meisha. Even the dark skin brotha nodded his head in agreement.

I turned and smiled at Meisha as she smiled and backed away.

I began again. "I umm, I agree with the brotha who yelled out that we needed more officers like myself to police our own neighborhoods. We can make that happen because one day all of this protesting and speaking out will pay off. So let's pretend for a minute that all of our hard work and shining a light on injustice have paid off tonight, right now. Let's say, somehow we finally have the attention of Louisiana's lawmakers, politicians, or even maybe the attention of the president of this country. Pretend that this major event takes place that forces our country to pay attention. What are we demanding from the leaders of this country?

"You, sistah in the front, what do you think?"

"Definitely equal school systems across the state. Schools where our Black and Brown kids will have the same success rate as the White schools or private schools. Also, I believe real authentic Black history should be taught in all schools or at the very least in the Black and Brown schools. These kids need to know the truth about their history in this country."

"Okay, good. What about you, brotha in the back?"

"Like I said before, we need more officers like yourself brotha to patrol our neighborhoods. Maybe the rate at which our families are dying by the hands of officers would decrease. And another damn thing is all of these liquor stores. There should be a limit of how many liquor stores are allowed in one area of our neighborhoods. My last suggestion is that these kids should be learning the importance of entrepreneurship or how important their credit score is instead of how Christopher Columbus stole this land."

"All of those ideas are important, so important that our ancestors have been fighting for some of the things mentioned their entire life. If I could add to those ideas from an officer's point of view, I would say equal sentencing would be major. This White racist system won't give their own harsh punishments and lock them away forever, so here's my proposal. Before our Black and Brown brothers or sisters receive judgment for crimes they're accused of, that brother or sister's situation should be compared to a White man or woman's sentencing for that same crime and vice versa. The punishment handed down to one race should not exceed the punishment of another unless one is a habitual offender.

"If we want to break down and rebuild this fucked-up system, we have to start with ourselves. From where we spend our money, what we allow to happen in our neighborhoods to how we treat one another. I believe we should buy Black and buy back our neighborhoods."

I looked over the crowd to my left, where a Caucasion sistah was standing and said, "No offense to our White members here tonight."

She smiled and said, "Any decent White sistah or brotha who is down for the cause would never take offense to that statement, Mr. Officer."

"Agreed, sistah. What's your name?"

"I'm Jessica."

Jessica was wearing a black headband tied across her blond dreadlocks and a black Bob Marley T-shirt.

"Well, I agree, Ms. Jessica. Our day will come sooner than we know it, my people. Until then, 'Buy Black and buy back.'"

I turned to Kevin as the members applauded. "They're all yours, bruh."

Kevin yelled, "All right, my people, let's work on our formations!"

He didn't have any military experience, but his father was a Marine, so he was in charge of teaching everyone military formations.

"Well, this went well," I said as I smiled and hugged Meisha, Derrick, and Joshua.

"You did well, brotha," Joshua stated.

"Thanks, I'm getting on the road. This long-ass ride home can get boring."

"I'll hit you up tomorrow, cuz," Derrick said as he turned to join Kevin.

As I prepared to drive away, I heard tapping on my passenger side window. It was Meisha waving her hand as I lowered the window.

"Derrick and the others are staying late tonight. Would you mind dropping me off uptown on your way out?" she asked.

"Of course not, get in," I offered.

Meisha sank down into the passenger's side of the car and smiled as she said, "Thanks. I promise I am marijuana free today."

"No worries, if you weren't I would have dropped your ass off at the jailhouse on my way home," I said with a straight face.

She leaned forward to get a look at my facial expression and said, "You wouldn't do that to me."

I smirked and replied, "Nah, I wouldn't. You hungry? I was going to stop by Jean's to get a po-boy on my way out."

"Yes, please. I haven't been there in a while."

"Meisha, I appreciate you holding me down tonight."

"Of course. Besides, dude was out of line for trying to expose you."

"How did you know he had weed in his car or that I didn't write him a ticket?"

We both turned and looked at each other and began laughing.

"Wild-ass guess, huh?"

"Hell yes, that fool smells like marijuana all the time. That wasn't a hard guess."

"Well, I appre…"

"Wait, look at this shit. It's always something around here." Meisha was pointing to a large crowd of people yelling at each other. "They're probably just fighting. Just keep going, Elijah. You don't need to get involved with this petty shit."

As I began to drive away, someone yelled, "He shot my brother!!"

I stopped the car and peered through the crowd. As some of the people began to disperse, I caught a glimpse of a girl seated on the ground screaming "He shot my brother" as she held her brother and pointed at a Black male standing over her. The Black male seemed angry and appeared to be yelling something at the female with the pistol still in his hand.

Before I knew it, I was standing outside of the car talking to Meisha through the window with my gun and badge in hand.

Meisha yelled, "What the hell are you thinking? This ain't the time to play super cop. Let's just go!!"

I yelled back, "Stay in the car, call the police, tell them that someone is shot and there is an officer here who needs backup! Say it just like that, Meisha!!"

I crept up close to the crowd and took cover behind the hood of an abandoned car. I took a deep breath to slow my accelerated heart rate before looking over the hood and yelling, "Police!! Let me see your hands!"

The handful of onlookers who were standing around turned their attention to me as they backed away from the gunman.

As the gunman turned to face me, I noticed he'd placed the gun inside his waistline.

"Police!! Put your fucking hands up!"

"Man fuck you, I ain't gotta do shit!" he yelled with his hands by his side.

My palms began sweating as I attempted to maintain the grip on my gun. I remembered thinking and battling with my conscience. *If I shoot, the media is gone have fun with this. This won't exactly help race relations amongst Black people either. Fuck it, I have to do what I have to do. Besides, he shot an unarmed man!!*

One of the onlookers yelled, "We all know how this shit ends. Another dead brotha shot by the pigs. Only difference this time is that it's a Black pig!"

He threw his hands up and shouted, "Come on and get you a kill, pig. White massa will sholl be proud of ya!!"

I repositioned my sweaty hands around my gun and refocused my aim on his chest. "Just keep your hands..."

My yelling was drowned out by sirens and sounds of the approaching police cars.

The look on the gunman's face changed from anger to confusion. With his hands in the air, he looked around at the crowd and then back to me. "Fuck!!" he screamed as he went to his knees with his hands in the air.

I quickly came from behind the car, removed his gun from his waistline, and placed it in mine. As I held him face down with his hands behind his back until backup arrived, I looked around at the mixed facial expressions in the crowd who had gathered around again. Some were relieved, some were just entertained, and others were angry.

I looked over to the sister holding her brother on the ground. He was conscious and breathing fine.

"So what now, Officer?" A Black male who wore a camouflage bandanna around his dreadlocks and looked to be in his mid-twenties stood over me waiting for a response to his question. "So what now? You get a nigga pig of the year award for this?" He looked around as he and a few others laughed.

My heart rate began rising again as I stood up and before I could weigh the consequence of my words, I said, "Nah, I ain't nobody's pig and for damn sure I ain't nobody's nigger. But you know what y'all problem is? Y'all don't value shit, and life is a joke to you. The fact that this brotha just put a bullet in another brotha for some dumbass reason is pure entertainment for y'all. Something is seriously wrong if you see a problem with me doing whatever it takes to save this brotha's life, no matter who's trying to take it. How the fuck does that help our communities if we continue to uplift and support the killers and drug dealers?! Look at this shit!"

I tucked my gun into my waistline, kneeled down, and began digging into the gunman's pockets. I pulled two clear plastic baggies of crack from his pocket and threw it on the ground.

"Look at this shit!! Now how did I know he had this shit?! He's selling dope and shooting his own people. But you call me a pig and a nigger!! If you have a problem with me taking this brotha to jail for him helping to eliminate our community, then y'all ain't as 'woke' as you claim to be."

No one was smiling. The angered and entertained facial expressions disappeared.

"So to answer your question, my man, nah I ain't looking to win no award. But y'all just look around, man. America wouldn't be America without us or our ancestors just as New Orleans wouldn't be New Orleans without us. From music, food, entertainment to the soul and vibe of the city, we are the source of it all, but we own next to nothing. Instead of demanding that we be allowed to enjoy the fruits of our labor, we help dig the grave for our culture and existence. Imagine where we could be if we supported one another before we supported anyone else. Imagine where our people would be as a whole if we decided to buy back our Black community and spend our money within our Black community!!"

"Sounds good to us, Mr. Officer!"

It was Meisha, along with Derrick and the rest of the group from the warehouse. I smiled and finally felt at ease.

"Sounds good to all of us, Mr. Officer. Buy Black and buy back!" Meisha began chanting and was soon joined by the rest of the group.

Buy Black, Buy Back!!
Buy Black, Buy Back!!
Buy Black, Buy Back!!

Backup finally arrived to take over, along with the ambulance. After giving all of the details to the investigating officer, Meisha and I disappeared from the scene as quickly as possible. Once back in the car, we spent the first five minutes of the ride home in silence. The radio was playing a heavy rotation of old school R&B, which she didn't seem to mind. Meisha buried her face into her phone as she slightly rocked from side to side to the rhythm of Maze's song "Happy Feelings" and other random songs that played.

"What cha know about this, Mr. Officer?" she said as she dropped her phone into her lap and turned the radio up. She sang with her hands in the air: "I liiiike the waaay, you kiss me when we're playin' the kissin' game!!"

I went from sneaking an occasional peek at her to having my eyes fixed on her more than the road ahead of me. I began admiring her beautiful dark skin and perfectly defined lips the same way I had when we first met. She was perfect. Strong-minded, naturally gorgeous, and on top of it all. Not to mention she could sing from what I was hearing.

"Can I have it back?!" she asked.

"Have what back?" I asked with a slight grin.

"My face, Mr. Officer. You know it's rude to stare."

We both laughed. "Yeah, you're right. Forgive me."

"You good!" she replied and picked up her phone.

"Before social media steals your attention away again, care to engage me in small talk, Meisha?"

"LOL, funny. Sure, what's up?"

Do you have an ole man? Can you be my girl? were the questions I asked in my head but didn't allow them to leave my mouth.

"Hello? What's on ya mind?" she asked as she lowered the volume on the music.

"Tell me some things about you that I don't know. I mean besides the obvious reason of wanting equality and justice, what would make a pretty girl like yourself leave the safety of her home to get her hands dirty in the streets?"

"Well, my mom..."

"Your mom was a part of a movement?" I interrupted.

"No, I was saying I first became interested in joining the movement in 2005 after my mother was murdered by three cops in New Orleans. It was a few days before Hurricane Katrina hit and caused a power outage in the city. My mother left home and went to the French Quarter to lock up her boutique shop. My younger brother and I waited for her to return home so that we all could leave the city before it was too late. She never returned home. Later that day, my uncle packed my brother and me into his van and drove us to Houston to escape the bad weather. I could remember sitting in the hotel room watching the news channels and seeing all of the bodies floating around the city streets. I convinced myself that somehow my mom made it out safely. Maybe she was one of those people stranded on top of the bridges waiting to be rescued. When the storm cleared and residents were allowed back into the city, myself, my uncle, three cousins and my brother all returned home. The city was totally dark and seemed like a scene from a horror movie. All attempts to locate my mom led to a dead-end until I convinced my uncle to visit my mother's shop. We didn't find my mom, but we were able to find video surveillance of her last visit to the shop. When we were able to view the video..."

I reached over and grabbed Meisha's hand as tears began to roll down her face. "I'm sorry, Meisha. Look, you don't have to talk about it if you don't want to. I should have never asked."

"No, it's fine," she said as she wiped the tears away and attempted to smile. "My mother was inside the shop preparing for the storm when three White officers walked through the front door. She began talking back and forth with the officers until the conversation seemed to become heated. The tallest of the officers who had a large tattoo on his forearm reached out and grabbed my mom. Her shirt ripped as she tried pulling away from the officer. The second cop was average height and kinda fat with a very thick mustache. He pulled her pants off as the first officer drug my mother to the rear of the store kicking and fighting the best she knew how. The third officer kept his face out of view of the camera for the most part. I could only see that he was just as tall as the first officer and had a scar on his right cheek. After the third officer locked the front door, the three officers took my mother out of view of the cameras and never returned to the front of the shop. The video footage ended there."

Meisha turned to me and said, "I'm no detective, Elijah, but I believe those officers harmed my mother."

Without taking my eyes off the road and too upset to look into her eyes, I mumbled, "I agree, Meisha. I agree. Of course this was reported to the authorities, right? What happened to those officers?" I asked as I glanced over to her.

"Sure we reported it. We even showed detectives the shop videos. They claimed that the video wasn't clear enough to identify the officers and it appeared that my mother was resisting the officers. After being turned away so many times and placing my mother on the lengthy list of missing persons, we received a call. My mom's body had been found burned to a crisp and was only identifiable by her dentures. For a long time afterwards once all of the tears dried up, I hated all policemen. White, Black, good or bad. I felt the system failed us as it always has. It for sure failed my mom. As for those officers, maybe they're retired with their feet up as if nothing never happened. Or maybe they're still patrolling Black neighborhoods and damaging lives. I will never forget their faces. The loud smell of cheap cologne one of the officers was wearing when they attacked my mom remained on her clothes, which were left behind in the shop. I keep her clothes in a plastic bag just to preserve the smell. Does that make me crazy?"

"Hell no, don't ever think that. You're super strong and braver than I thought. To say you're holding everything together after all you've been through is beyond amazing. It seems to me that most, if not all Blacks are able to tell a story of tragedy and/or life changing events, which altered their life one way or another."

"I agree," said Meisha. "So what's your story? What made a young Black man from the hood become an officer?"

"Faith, I guess. I never had plans of becoming a police officer when I was young. No one in my family had ever become one. It was just a choice I made later in life. It has proven to be one of the best decisions I've ever made. I mean, despite the reputation officers have, being an officer allowed me to see both sides of the fence. All of the ways in which racist America mistreats and oppresses our people becomes that much clearer on this side of the fence. Just as all the ways our people continue to allow themselves to be oppressed is just as clear. I believe the biggest assumption our people have about Black officers is that you have to somehow betray who you are to become an officer. One thing I am proud of is that I have never betrayed myself as a man or a Black man to hold this position I'm in. It has only made me wiser and more disciplined.

"Well, anyway, Meisha. We are your family now and I believe everything happens for a reason. There is a reason we all came together to fight this battle. We have to push forward and stick around long enough to find out why."

"That's me on the left," Meisha stated as she pointed to a yellow duplex apartment.

She reached out and hugged me tight. "Wow, I never would've guessed I would become close friends with a cop," she stated as we both smiled. "Everything happens for a reason, right? Let's push forward and see what happens, Mr. Officer."

"Good night, Meisha."

On my drive back home, my statement to Meisha replayed over in my head. "We are your family now." It was true.

After that eventful night, the days seemed to pass by swiftly. It's been a year since Derrick introduced me to Meisha, Kevin, and Joshua. Since then, we've come to know nearly everything about one another. I guess being loyal to finding a way to rise above oppression brought us close together. What's most comforting to me is the fact that after all this time my new "family" has allowed me to live a sort of double life without exposing me or treating me any differently. I haven't heard of many officers who could actually say he/she fought for justice and what was right both in and out of uniform. The thought of it made the hairs on my arm stand tall and gave me chills knowing that if anyone found out I would be fired immediately. It wouldn't matter that I was fighting for the exact same "justice for all" that I fought for while in uniform. The thought of it also made my heart rate rise and put a smile on my face simultaneously. If the lower class, underprivileged and oppressed people of Louisiana ever had a secret weapon, I was it.

CHAPTER SEVEN

THERE ARE TIMES WHEN THE END JUSTIFIES THE MEANS

A MASTER IS INCAPABLE OF HEARING THE CRIES OF HIS SERVANTS.

The hallway was dark, and the only visible light came from beneath the bathroom door. It was late at night, and I was six years old inside of my grandmother's roach-infested three-bedroom apartment on the West Bank of New Orleans. My older sister, older cousin, and I were up late watching cartoons in our room. I continuously peeped out of the door down the dark hallway at the bathroom door, waiting for my turn to use it. My grandmother's boyfriend had been inside for some time, and I couldn't hold it any longer. I reluctantly walked down the dark hallway and knocked at the bathroom door, which he quickly opened. "I have to use it," I said, holding my wiener to be sure nothing leaked out. While looking down at me, he stepped aside to let me in. I rushed to the toilet to relieve myself as he closed the door behind me. Once done, I went over to the sink to wash my hands. He picked me up so that I could reach the faucet. As I turned the water on, he was grabbing my pajama pants and pulling them down. I didn't understand why he needed to pull my pants down, but before I could react, I felt him inside of me. My sister and cousin began abruptly knocking at the bathroom door, which caused him to stop whatever it was he was doing to me.

As they knocked again, he yelled, "He's hiding!" Without saying a word to me, he pulled my pajama pants up and released me back out into the dark hallway. At that moment, I wasn't sure what to think or how to feel, so I returned to my room with my sister and older cousin, where I buried my face in the cartoons as if I was the same boy that left the room to pee. The truth was that now, there was an unknown hole in my heart. I would never be the same.

The blaring 4 am alarm snatched me out of my deep sleep and away from the series of unfortunate memories that I had often wished I had the ability to forget. It had been a while since I'd dreamt about that time in my life, but when I did, it never failed to bring about a different series of emotions. Somewhere between being drenched in sweat and an overflow of various feelings, I always seemed to end with the most grateful and humbling thoughts. The byproduct of trauma is different for each of us. For me, it served to cultivate me into a human being with immense compassion for others and a quest to be sensitive to and aware of the circumstances surrounding the decisions a person makes prior to placing judgment upon their actions.

I kept these thoughts in mind as I prepared for work, spending more time than usual in front of the mirror with my toothbrush in hand examining myself. My body and mind had become so accustomed to popping up and preparing for work, I hardly had to give the notion of grace any thought, although it was a part of my DNA and approach towards policing. By the time I was dressed and in my police car, I received a text message from my lieutenant.

Stop by my office when you get in.

I threw the phone onto the passenger's seat and thought that I needed a cup of coffee before I could deal with the bullshit. Around the force, we referred to it as liquid crack.

I stopped at the gas station next to the office to get a cup of crack in a cup. It was a little after 6 am, which allowed me the time to sit in my police car until The Breakfast Club came on the radio. Between writing tickets and working car crashes, I never had time to catch up on current events outside of crime. The Breakfast Club was like a one-stop shop for me.

DJ Envy, Charlamagne Tha God, and Angela Yee handed out the Rumor Report, top stories in the news, and gave a deserving soul "Donkey of the Day for acting like an ass, an award I felt was most often earned. The moment to bask in something outside of work ended far too soon.

When I pulled up to the office to speak with the lieutenant, my cup was nearly empty. Before I could get through the front door, I heard someone yell, "What's up, lil brotha?!"

That can only be one person, I thought as I looked back and saw Dennis leaning out of the window of his police car as he left the parking lot. It was obvious that his shift was over, and he was going home with a big smile on his face.

I smiled and shook my head as I entered the lieutenant's office.

"Morning, Steele!"

"Morning, sir. You needed to see me?"

"Yeah, you have been subpoenaed to show in court this morning for 9 am. It's for two different cases. Do the names James Riley and Milton Collins ring a bell?"

"Yes. I caught James Riley after he stole food and a few clothing items from the downtown supermarket. That wasn't his first time. Milton Collins decided to get high on methamphetamines, steal his neighbor's vehicle, and take us on a high speed chase throughout Bigot. Why'd you ask?"

He took his reading glasses off, which were resting on the edge of his nose, and sat them on his desk. "That Milton kid is a good kid, ya know. I spoke with his dad today. Do you know his dad?"

"No sir."

"Frank Collins is his dad. Frank owns an offshore company here in Bigot. He's the reason our department is able to afford all of this new equipment. Shit, not only that, but he sponsors all of our golf tournaments."

I sat quiet…

"Now you know I wouldn't ever tell you how to do your job. You're young, with a bright future ahead of you, and I trust your judgment, Elijah.

I know you'll do the right thing," he stated with a cheap-ass car salesman smirk on his face.

"Well, I appreciate the heads-up, Lieutenant. I'll be there at 9 am."

Before I left the office, I sat at the front desk and printed out all of the evidence associated with both Riley's and Collins' cases. Body camera video, store surveillance video, and witness statements. I wasn't the most organized, but the flash drive I kept in my top pocket was like a file cabinet.

After that convo with the lieutenant, there was no telling what type of foolery was unfolding. Either way, I wanted to cover my ass. I had heard stories of other officers doing favors, but it had nothing to do with me. For me to go into a courtroom and mess up my credibility for someone who didn't give two fucks about me or himself was foolish.

"Please give this white jar of mayonnaise the biggest hee haw!!"

Truer words couldn't have been spoken. I was back in the car just in time to hear the Donkey of the Day for myself. And because he made mention of a jar of mayonnaise, I knew that this award had gone to some-one White. I could also deduce that whomever had been awarded was likely from the state of Florida as they seemed to be the overall winners according to Charlamagne's renderings. Had Charlamagne known about what I was currently experiencing, he might have given the award to my lieutenant. *Oh well*, I thought. *Let the shit show begin.*

I arrived at the courthouse around 8:27 am. The judges never arrived in the courtroom before 9. I only knew that because of the two years I'd spent working in the jailhouse. The inmates who had been taken to jail the day before were all retrieved from the holding cell one by one to be seen by the judge for 8 am.

Standing just outside, I thought to myself, *God is good, and I thank Him for my progression.*

Although I appreciated the experience of working in the jailhouse, I didn't miss it.

Both Riley's and Collins' cases were fresh on my brain, and I still remembered all the details of both cases, which meant that reading over my reports briefly was sufficient enough for my testimony in court. James Riley was a thirty-four-year-old Black guy who had been caught stealing from the same supermarket on several occasions. While on our way to jail after I arrested Riley, he explained to me that he was bringing the groceries he stole home to his grandmother and little brother. As I listened to Riley talk, I read over his criminal history. He had only been arrested for a misdemeanor theft of goods but nothing major that would make him a violent offender or cause him to be sentenced to a long stint in prison. I remember immediately thinking, "Here's another case that would cause me to question my authenticity as a Black officer, right?"

I recalled feeling like shit from the moment Riley shared his circumstances with me from the backseat of my patrol car with his hands behind his back and his head hung low in shame. Was I a hypocrite? I remember a young boy who was without his mother or father. A boy who woke up early many mornings without anything to eat. A boy who walked into the same convenience store on the West Bank of New Orleans and shoved bacon & eggs down his pants before walking out, only to bring the bacon & eggs back home to rumbling stomachs. Rationalizing with myself about why I had to take Riley to jail for doing what he did was something I chose not to attempt. However, I vowed to never place myself in a situation to make myself feel this way again.

Milton Collins' case also had an effect on me. Collins was a twenty-eight-year-old White guy who had a drug problem. Methamphetamines were his drug of choice, and the city of Bigot was known for it, but Collins' family's wealth gave him access to any and every pill his heart desired. His family's wealth also seemed to grant him freedom from prison each time. I had a front row seat to Collins' arrogance and White privilege after I arrested him for theft of a motor vehicle and aggravated flight from an officer, two felonies. No-good people come in all shapes, sizes and races, Black, White, pink, or purple, but no matter the race, Collins was my favorite person to arrest. My chin was always held high with pride amidst his entire transport to the jailhouse. The loud yelling of, "You ain't shit, nigger," or, "I can buy you," was always drowned out by the most "Black" and Afrocentric music I could find in my playlist. In Collins' case, he was often blessed by Kendrick Lamar's album *To Pimp A Butterfly*. The song "The Blacker The Berry" in particular remained on repeat.

While driving, I nodded my head and snuck the occasional peak into my rearview mirror to see the disgust on his face as he stared out the window. If Collins' thoughts at that very moment were for sale, I would pay top dollar to gain access. It had to be torture for someone like him to have his freedom temporarily taken away from him by a Black man. On top of that, to sit handcuffed in the rear of my police truck being serenaded by lyrics infused with Black pride. A whirlwind indeed.

I reached back into the car and grabbed my clip-on tie and reports off the passenger's seat before walking up the courthouse steps. Inside, the noisy hallways were filled with people of all ages and races, all waiting to either pay traffic tickets or answer to the judge for the crimes they had supposedly committed. They all were lined against both sides of the hallway walls waiting to pass through the metal detector which led into the actual courtroom. It never failed. As soon as I hit the hallway, all eyes were on the guy with the uniform and shiny badge. I believe I have perfected a look just for this because I revert back to it every time I am in this situation. Straight-faced, no smile or frown, but a face that was ready to go either way.

"Wazzam New Orleans?"

I stopped pretending to be reading over my report and lifted my head up to find this tall White dude speaking to me. The nicknames "New Orleans" and "Shorty" were given to me by the inmates when I worked in Bigot's jailhouse. *Ricky something*, I thought to myself as I tried to remember his full name. I dapped him off and asked, "What's good, Rick? You been coolin'?"

"Yeah, Shorty man, I found a job and got married," he said as he pointed to the young lady beside him.

"How ya doing?" I asked his wife as I smiled and shook her hand. I turned back to him with a smile on my face as confirmation that he was doing good. "That's what's up, Rick."

"Ay, you came a long way since the jail, Shorty. Keep climbing, bruh. That's a good dude, bae," Rick whispered to his wife as I walked away.

An older Black woman, who was most likely there to support a family member, smiled as I walked past her and said, "That is a blessing. That's all right, young man."

I smiled and continued walking. I knew exactly what she meant. Maybe it's just me, but it seems no matter where you're from, Black mothers and grandmothers speak a universal language when they are proud of you. She approved of me and my work ethic, which was proven by her sincere smile.

"It must be jelly 'cause jam don't shake like that."

Here comes the homosexual jokes, I thought to myself as I walked up to the metal detectors.

Someone whispered in an exaggerated deep voice, "Strip, lil nigga!!"

There's only one clown who would play with me like that, I thought as I stepped through the metal detectors to see Brian smiling from ear to ear.

I dapped Brian off.

"Bruh, I knew it was you. When did you start working up here?"

"I was moved out of the jail about a year ago. I got tired of sitting in that place, man. Felt like I was doing time instead of working. Besides, pulling sporks out of people's butts gets old."

"That's cold, man."

"Who are you here for?"

"James Riley and Milton Collins."

"Let me guess, James stealing out of the store again. I went to school with James. He was a real smart dude, always on the honor roll. I guess when his mom and dad went to prison, things started going downhill.

And Milton Collins? Why you show up for that shit anyway? His family already bought the district attorney and judge. Good luck, brotha, they are already seated inside of the courtroom."

"Thanks, man. Good seeing you, brotha."

I walked into the nearly empty courtroom and caught the attention of the people when the noisy door closed behind me. James Riley and his family were seated on the left side of the room near the middle. I glanced at them and continued to make my way to the front where there was reserved seating for officers and took my seat.

"Officer Steele?"

"Yes, sir. I'm Steele."

"Nice to meet you, sir. I'm district attorney George Freeman. I'll be handling both of your cases today. Just to let you know where we're going with this. We want so bad to make this thing stick to Milton Collins, but we don't seem to have hardcore evidence to bring the case home."

"Hardcore evidence? What about the dashcam video and bodycam video which shows everything?!"

"The video files were damaged when we attempted to make copies to show in court. Trust me, we have tried to exhaust all avenues to get the video copied, but without those videos this case isn't strong enough to convict. Now, this Riley fellow, we have dealt with him twice before after he has stolen goods from the supermarket. He clearly doesn't get it. I believe the best thing to do in his case is to hit him with a habitual offender and offer ten years minimum."

"What?! No!" I said in a strong whisper. "Wait," I said as Freeman got up and walked away.

"All rise," the court officer yelled. "Court is now in session. Honorable Judge Margaret Dobbins presiding."

"Be seated please. Are there any resolved matters to be heard first?"

"Yes, your honor." Freeman stepped forward. "We have the matter of James Riley. Mr. Riley and his attorney public defender Jeremy Stevenson are present today."

James stood behind his attorney looking like a lost soul who didn't have a clue.

"Your honor, Mr. Riley and his attorney are prepared to accept a plea deal of ten years for Mr. Riley if he pleads guilty today. Mr. Riley is a habitual offender, therefore, we believe he should be charged accordingly."

First my neck got hot. Then my feet became warmer and my heart rate suddenly elevated. I felt myself becoming upset. This was some bullshit, and it seemed as if James' attorney was all for it.

"Your honor." I jumped to my feet and before I knew it, I was walking to the middle of the courtroom. "Excuse me, your honor."

"Officer, would you please have a seat and wait your time."

"Ma'am, I am the investigating officer in this case. I believe there's a mistake being made here that would cause Mr. Riley to face an unjustifiable conviction. According to the way Louisiana classifies a habitual offender, Mr. Riley's case does not come close. He has been arrested on several occasions and accused of stealing goods from the supermarket, but he has only been convicted once for a misdemeanor offense. Besides that one conviction, your honor, Mr. Riley's criminal history is blemish free."

"What are you doing?" Freeman turned and asked. "Have a seat and let me do my job, Steele."

"Is this true, Mr. Freeman?"

"Ughh yes, Your Honor, but…"

"Mr. Riley, how much time did you spend in jail after being arrested, sir?"

I nudged James with my elbow. "Tell her."

James lifted his head. "Three days, ma'am."

"Credit for time served. You're dismissed, son. I hope to never see you in my courtroom again."

I heard a loud celebratory "Yes" among the chatter in the courtroom. I assumed it was James' grandmother, but I didn't turn to look. James smiled at me before walking out.

"Mr. Freeman, let's be sure to not make any more mistakes such as this one, sir. As for you, Officer Steele, please refrain from interrupting my courtroom."

Milton Collins smiled and winked his eye at me as I took my seat.

"Mr. Freeman, any more cases we should address first sir?"

"Yes, your honor, we would like to call forward the case of Milton Collins. Mr. Collins was arrested and accused of stealing a vehicle, consuming drugs, and taking officers on a high speed chase. As horrible as this sounds, Your Honor, I don't believe we possess enough evidence to convict Mr. Collins. With damaged video footage, we're only left with the officer's words against Collins' words. We would be left with trying the case based on hearsay. As the district attorney, I move to dismiss all charges against Mr. Collins."

My lieutenant had to be responsible for damaging my bodycam and dash-cam video, I thought. I placed my hand over the top pocket of my shirt and felt Collins' future at the tip of my fingers. I looked over at Collins, who winked at me once again. I immediately smiled and winked back. The smile disappeared as he began to squirm, wondering what I was up to.

Refrain from interrupting my courtroom, I thought as I contemplated standing up again.

Instead, I raised my hand high in the air.

"What is it, Mr. Steele? Is this your case as well?"

"Yes, Your Honor. I am the investigating officer of this case as well."

"Unless you have evid…"

I pulled my flash drive from my top pocket and raised it high. "Here's a copy of my dash camera video and body camera video."

Freeman looked as if he wanted to die and disappear from the courtroom. "What are you? Would you just sit your ass down?!"

Chatter in the courtroom became louder. "Order!! Order in this courtroom!!" the judge yelled.

"If the court would allow it, here's proof that Milton Collins placed the citizens of Bigot in danger by fleeing officers in a stolen vehicle."

"Bailiff, if you would please."

Brian stepped forward and took the flash drive from me. "Nigga, you a dead man," he whispered jokingly.

The video was placed on a projection screen for the entire court to see. Two minutes into the video, Judge Dobbins stated: "I have seen enough. Mr. Freeman, I need to see you in my chambers now. Officer Steele, you're free to go, sir. Court is now in recess. Bailiff, detain Mr. Collins until we return."

Milton's father stood to his feet. I glanced over at him as I exited the courtroom. "Freeman, how could you allow this to happen?!" he yelled. "You better fix this, Freeman!"

I exited the courtroom smiling from ear to ear.

My phone vibrated as I began to drive away from the courthouse. It was a text message from my lieutenant.

Report to my office ASAP!!

I tossed my phone on my passenger seat. It was at that moment that I knew what my momma meant when she said, "If it ain't one thing it's another."

CHAPTER EIGHT

NEW GENERATION. NEW REVOLUTION.

DIMMED FLAMES DON'T ILLUMINATE SOULS.

"Steele, come in and have a seat," my lieutenant stated without taking his eyes off of the muted television in his office.

I could tell by the flush redness which took over his usual pale skin tone that he was upset. *It's obvious he's received a call from Frank Collins about what took place in court,* I thought to myself. *Oh well, wouldn't be the first time he's been pissed off. What the fuck can he do, fire me?*

My facial expression soon matched the stale and impatient look he had on his face. I sat down and waited for him to speak.

"Can you explain this shit to me?" he asked as he pointed to the television.

When I turned and faced the television, my stomach began to tighten to the point of discomfort, and my throat was suddenly dry, or at least it felt that way. Someone had recorded the incident that took place the night before, and now the incident was all over the local news channels.

Without adjusting my facial expression, I calmly responded, "I was in the area when that shooting took place sir, so I reacted just as any other officer would have reacted."

"Yeah, you reacted just fine, you did exactly what you were trained to do. It was all perfect, except when you became a fucking psychiatrist and a civil rights activist after identifying yourself as an officer. I mean, here you are on a goddamn shooting scene telling people where to spend their money and how to live their lives! If they want to shoot and kill one another, that's their problem, don't make it yours. Last time I checked, Steele, the department didn't train you or pay you to be the next Martin Luther King Jr. or whoever the fuck you thought you were being out there. You're here to enforce the goddamn law, Steele. Nothing more, nothing less. Just do your damn job and go home." After screeching, he turned back towards me and said, "And when were you going to tell me about this incident anyway?"

"Well, today, sir," I said calmly.

"The day is almost over!"

"I was blind-sided by those two court cases from this morning, sir," as I continued to maintain eye contact and noticed that he wasn't buying into the lie I'd just told. I was hoping to keep the incident a secret, and he knew it.

"How about you go ahead and take the rest of the day off so you won't be blind-sided by anything else. This should give you a little time to figure out if your loyalty is with the department or elsewhere."

Without saying a word, I stood up and opened the office door to leave when he stopped me.

"Speaking of loyalty to the department, Frank Collins called me and he was not pleased with what you did to his son in court today. I told you how important his contributions are to this department. What the hell happened?!"

"Well..." I said with a grin, "I did my job and now I'm going home."

I left the office with my head held high and headed home.

While sitting on my couch processing the series of events, I was alerted by a text. *When you make it big, don't forget about the rest of us.* It was Meisha.

Lol, what are you talking about? I replied.

Last night's incident has taken off on social media. Everyone seems to think what you did was cool. The video has over two million views and the hashtag #BUYBLACK&BUYBACK have been posted over a million times.

Well, that didn't take long. I guess I ain't too surprised. My supervisor was pissed when he seen the incident on television and gave me the rest of the day off, I wrote back.

Sorry that happened, but you might as well make the best of it. Derrick and Josh are on their way to my crib now. Come chill with us?? I cooked!!

She had me convinced with the food. I wasn't up for the drive, but I was starved, and the grilled cheese sandwich that I was capable of making for myself wasn't gonna work. Besides I didn't have anything else to do, and chillin with the fellas and Meisha was the next best thing.

A few hours later I pulled up to Meisha's apartment and noticed Derrick's truck wasn't there yet. Maybe he and Josh had been sent to the store for something. Meisha's front door was cracked open enough to where I could hear her singing and smell what she was cooking before I could close my car door.

"Yooo!!" I said as I knocked at the slightly opened door. I peeped in and saw Meisha standing in the kitchen, singing and prepping food. She looked up as I stepped through the door.

"Oh, what's up, Elijah? Come in, I didn't hear you knocking. Make yourself comfortable…you hungry?"

Meisha's apartment had that old school Black auntie house feel to it from the family portraits on the wall and the television mixed in with the portraits of Black women wearing African head wraps. The head wraps were similar to the one Meisha was wearing as she danced around the kitchen. She even had the brown peacock chair that was notorious in Black homes. The same one in the famous Huey P. Newton picture where he's dressed in all black holding a rifle in one hand and a spear in the other.

"Yeah, I can eat a lil bit," I replied.

'A lil bit' is what I say when I'm being modest and eating food prepared by someone for the first time. Even though I knew it was bullshit cause I was starving, but I didn't want a plate full if the food wasn't good, and I had no way of knowing yet.

In true New Orleans fashion, Meisha handed me a full plate of cornbread dressing, macaroni & cheese, potato salad, and a bowl of gumbo.

I quickly went to work on the food as Meisha cleaned the kitchen, sung along and slow danced to what I assumed was her personal playlist of songs.

"Where everybody at?" I asked Meisha.

"Josh and Derrick had to go handle some business. They didn't give any details so I didn't ask."

"Right, everything's a secret with Derrick."

"No worries, though, you're safe in my house. I won't hurt you," Meisha said with a slight grin without missing a beat in her two-step.

"What?!" I laughed. "Girl, ain't nobody worried about you."

She was right, I was safe. At least I felt that way. I always had the space to be myself around her and the fellas, and that was cool. No police officer, no looking over my shoulder, just me. A switch was flipped when I was with them. I could laugh out loud and express my feelings without judgment. I was only required to be the purest form of myself, and it was invaluable to me.

Even so, Meisha was a disrupter. She had this weird way of finding that thing that makes you most uneasy. Before you felt any resentment towards her she would have you feeding off of her energy until you were back at ease.

"Aww man, I love this song." Meisha turned the volume up to Musiq Soulchild's "Love" and began slowly rocking side to side with her hands in the air until motioning for me to come towards her.

"Dance with me please?!!" she begged.

"Nah, I'm good. I don't dance," I said as I tried looking serious.

"Please dance with me," she asked again with an exaggerated sad puppy look on her face. "You gone make me beg?"

Before I could respond, she grabbed my hand, making me stand up. She placed my hands around her waist while I stared down at my own feet to be sure I didn't step on her toes or slippers.

Meisha smiled. "What are you looking at?"

"I'm trying not to crush your pretty little feet. Besides I don't want to be all in your face with this gumbo on my breath," I joked nervously.

"It won't kill me."

We rocked slowly and stared at one another until I felt myself pulling her closer. I could feel every rapid beat of Meisha's heart from the time it sped up and slowed down. As her heart rate fell back to normal, she laid her head on my shoulder.

"Are you okay?" I asked.

"I am now." She sighed deeply. "I've never been held like this before."

"That's hard to believe."

"What's that supposed to mean?"

"I mean no disrespect, but I assume you've had a man before right?"

"Yeah, so what? Just being with a man doesn't teach him how to love and care for you. Especially if he isn't willing to learn, ya know?"

"Understood. It seems to me that loving you would be easy. From the outside looking in, you appear to be full of love. Even behind that rebel mask you put on when you walk out your door."

Meisha stopped rocking and lifted her head off my shoulder.

"Thank you. That was sweet, but most guys run when they see what's behind the mask or what scars and baggage that a woman may be carrying."

"Not all men. You just have to find a man who is willing to embrace your scars."

"What would you do with a woman with scars?"

"Depends on what kind of woman we're talking about."

"My kind of woman. What would you do with my scars?"

"I would probably kis…" I pulled Meisha in closer to me until my lips met hers. The fast pace of both our hearts beating in our chests did not match the slow motion in which we kissed one another. We locked lips and traded tongues as if this was our last kiss and the world would end tonight. Meisha had to be feeling my now fully erect penis which was lying against my right thigh and being pressed against what I assumed was her zipper. The respect Meisha demanded as a woman kept me from pushing this moment any further. Until she suddenly pushed both of my hands down to her soft ass and whispered....

"Have you ever made love, Officer?"

"Yeah, I guess," I said without breaking eye contact with Meisha.

"Show me how that feels," Meisha said before she wrapped her arms around my neck and began kissing me again.

Her legs wrapped around me when I lifted her off the floor and began walking to the back bedroom. Meisha's playlist was rolling and didn't miss a beat. Keri Hilson's "Love" began to play as we quietly undressed each other. The light from beneath the closet door allowed me to catch glimpses of Meisha's different facial expressions. I laid her down on the bed and watched closely as her expression changed from eager to concern. As I kissed her stomach just below her breast, Meisha placed her hands just below her navel and above her vagina as if she wanted to hide something. I knew exactly what it was. She lifted her head off the bed to watch me as I slowly removed her hands and began kissing the scar she'd tried covering. She gave me the blessing to proceed by placing her hands on my head as she laid her head down on the bed again. Meisha gasped and gripped the sheets as my tongue slowly slid up and down continuously across her clitoris. She thanked me by leaving evidence of gratitude on my chin. We were back kissing again, only this time I was pushing my tongue in and out of her lips below.

Meisha pulled me up to her when she grew tired of her legs quivering and shaking. She wiped the creamy gratitude from my lips as she stared in my eyes as if she wondered what was next. I kissed her lips, put her legs on my shoulders, and slid slowly inside her. She gripped the back of my arms as I slid in and out without going too deep.

"Don't stop," Meisha gasped as a tear rolled down the side of her face. She put her hands on my butt and pulled me in deeper.

We both visualized the finish line when Meisha climbed on top and began grinding. Her legs were quivering again. I was focused on keeping my toes from curling amidst the warmth of being inside her. Before we knew it, we were both lying on our backs staring at the ceiling. Meisha rolled over into my right arm and laid her head onto my chest. We lay quietly, finally gaining control of our breathing. I held her and caressed her thigh before running my fingers across the scar below her navel. She didn't flinch. Instead she looked up at me and asked, "Do you wanna know?"

"Wanna know what?" I asked.

She held her hand on top of mine and rubbed my fingers across her scar again. "Do you want to know how I got it?"

I kissed her forehead and said, "I'm listening."

"After I returned to the city to look for my mom, I learned I was pregnant. Looking back on it, I was so young that I didn't know how to feel about it. I was confused, I was sad, alone and scared. I even felt dirty at times. My uncle somehow thought it was a good idea to take advantage of my mother not being around. He had sex with me several times while we were away for the storm. I couldn't wait to get back to tell my mom what he had been doing to me. She would've kicked his ass, and he knew it. But instead of finding her I was stuck with unanswered questions and an illegitimate child on the way. A child whom I was prepared to love unconditionally had he survived. During my pregnancy I was always stressed and mad that my no good uncle was the only family I knew to take me to my doctors' visits, where for some reason I pretended that he didn't violate me. Complications during the pregnancy led me to having a Caesarean section, and my child was stillborn. Some days this scar is very important to me as it symbolizes life that once was. Other days I am ashamed and regretful."

Meisha went on to say, "No one ever made me feel this secure and confident about it. I appreciate you for that."

"I identify with your pain in more ways than you know, Meisha. Your strength amazes me."

"How did you get rid of the pain inside of you, Elijah?"

"Sometimes I don't feel as if the pain is totally gone. Before I got to the point I'm at now, staying busy was my temporary remedy to the pain. Too much time sitting and thinking was a sure way of the pain returning one way or another. I am in more control of it now than I have ever been."

"How does that feel?" Meisha lifted her head and asked.

"How does what feel?"

"To have control over your pain?"

"It feels like a huge accomplishment. It feels like a weight being constantly lifted. That weight sometimes returns with the racism I deal with as an officer. Racism from the public and from the department I work for."

"Hmm, interesting. How does that feel? To deal with racism in uniform and out of uniform?"

"Sometimes that shit deals with itself, Meisha. I couldn't tell you how many times I have ran into someone White who believed they were entitled to receive a warning for a speeding ticket. Or one who didn't believe I could take them to jail because I was Black. Well until they realized I didn't have that back on the plantation mentality and they were in handcuffs. Don't get me wrong, Meisha, not all White citizens have acted inappropriately and not all officers are fucked up. But enough of them are fucked up, and the officers that aren't don't do shit about the dirty ones. Even the good Black officers who have no reason to be loyal to the rotten officers are often publicly quiet about these fucked-up officers and departments. They remain quiet and rather suffer through an entire career of being shit on, passed over, and being treated like robots instead of speaking up. Their biggest fear is losing their career or being passed over for promotions, which happens anyway."

"That's stressful, Elijah. When does our pain go away or will it ever go away?" Meisha whispered as she yawned and snuggled her head up close to my chest.

"Well....shit, I really don't have a solid answer for that. I guess sometimes when you've exhausted all other reasonable means, the only thing left to do is pinpoint that thing that pains you the most and eliminate it from your life the best way you know how."

Meisha didn't respond. Instead she repositioned her body next to mine and fell off into a deep sleep.

CHAPTER NINE

THE PRICE OF CHAINS AND SLAVERY

DIMMED FLAMES DON'T ILLUMINATE SOULS.

The next morning, the squeaky sound that came from Meisha turning the knob to start her shower startled me from my sleep. I sat up in the bed and tried rubbing my face in an attempt to wake myself all the way up before attempting to exit the bed. *Her light bill is going to be high,* I thought to myself while staring over at the closet light that was left on from the night before. After slipping my pants on, I reached inside of the closet to pull the light string. Something in me said *Look up.* There was a bag with a note on it that read *Mommy.* My heart began to race, and I remembered Meisha saying that she kept the clothes left behind in her mother's shop after her mother was attacked. My curiosity wouldn't allow me to leave without grabbing the bag to get a closer look at the items. When I heard Meisha turn the shower off I quickly returned the bag to the top shelf of the closet, turned the light off, and closed the door. Meisha walked into the bedroom just as I put on my shoes.

"Hey, big head, do you want breakfast?" she asked.

"Nah, I need to get home and get cleaned up. I have a few things that need to be taken care of today."

Meisha hugged me and said, "Well, thank you for caring. Thanks for umm, everything."

"Nah, thank you. You're a reminder of how strong and beautiful our Black queens can be. Even in the midst of the bullshit. But I just can't believe you're around here making love to a police officer," I said jokingly.

Meisha laughed as she pushed me backwards into her dresser. "Don't make me kick your ass, punk."

We both laughed. I leaned over to pick up what looked like a passport that had fallen from the dresser when I bumped it.

"You planning a trip?" I asked Meisha.

"No, but you never know. One day I may just want to get away from here," she replied. "Where would you go if you wanted to get away for a while?"

"Cuba," I replied quickly.

"That didn't take you long. Did you wake up with Cuba on your mind?"

"Nah, I honestly don't know much about Cuba, but I would love to meet Assatta Shakur. Just to have a simple conversation with her, ya know?"

"That would be so dope," she replied.

Meisha placed her passport back on her dresser as I walked toward the front door.

"Don't forget to write!!" Meisha said with a big smile on her face.

"Write? Is that your way of telling me to text you later?"

"Figure it out, Officer!"

I laughed and leaned in for a kiss but was met with the palm of Meisha's hand.

"No sir. No more gumbo breath. Go take care of that."

We both laughed as I walked out of the house.

I arrived at my apartment to clean myself up and feed my face. The steam from the shower eventually turned my bathroom into a sauna as I stood deep in thought while the hot water poured over my head. My mind took me back to Meisha's closet. Her mom was heavy on my thoughts. I wanted badly to help Meisha receive some type of closure and justice.

Fuck it, I thought to myself. I finished up in the shower, ate a quick meal, and was back in the car on the road to Baton Rouge.

Christine, who is a part of our agency's forensics team, owed me a favor, and I was on my way to collect on it. While on her probationary hiring period with our agency, she'd received a speeding ticket while in Bigot. I called in a favor to help her keep her job.

When I arrived, Christine, a petite White chick, was standing at the front counter filing paperwork with her back to me. Her small stature and signature pink highlights confirmed her identity before she turned to face me. It had been a while since I'd seen her in person. Any evidence to be submitted to the lab is usually submitted back at our office through our evidence custodian. Obviously this could not wait.

"What's up, chick?" I said with a slight grin.

Christine squinted her eyes, pushed her pink glasses snug upon her face, and smiled. "Heeey, stranger!" she said in an excited whisper. "What brings you up here?"

I set the plastic bag on top of the counter without saying a word.

"Okay, where's the rest of it? This isn't even properly packaged. No paperwork?" Christine asked sarcastically.

Again, without saying a word, I just shook my head. Christine noticed my serious facial expression and began to look around to see if anyone was watching her.

"All right, I got it. I'll text you when I'm done with everything."

"Thanks a lot," I said as I turned and began to walk out.

"Hey, be careful out there," Christine said. "Did you hear about the shooting this morning?"

"Nah," I said with a curious look on my face.

"Well, about thirty minutes before you walked in, we got word that a local officer shot a kid in the back near Mckinley and Georgia Street. It doesn't sound good at all, so I'm sure you'll be hearing about it."

"Aight, thanks, Christine."

I remember feeling heavier after walking out of the forensic lab than I did when I entered. It almost felt like I was digging a hole for myself. My lieutenant was already on my ass, and now I was submitting 'off the record' evidence. On top of that, if Meisha found out that I took shit from her home without asking she was gonna flip out. I thought, *Maybe she'll be able to forgive me if Christine is able to find some concrete evidence.*

The pressure was weighing heavily on me mentally and getting worse as the day progressed. I got back into my car and saw I had a missed call from Derrick. Guess he'd decided to come out of hiding.

When I called him back, he answered on the second ring.

"Glad you decided to reappear," I said jokingly.

"We can address that later," Derrick said in a serious tone. "It's go time. These motherfuckers have shot a young kid in the back in Baton Rouge."

"Yeah, I heard, but do we know all of the details before we jump to conclusions?"

"That's where you come in, Mr. Officer. You find out the details and we'll be on our way to Baton Rouge. Will you be there?" Derrick asked just as I was getting a notification for another call. I looked at the screen to see who it was and confirmed that it was my lieutenant.

"I'll call you back, Derrick."

I could have guessed what my lieutenant wanted. It was just an uneasy feeling I had.

"Yes, sir? What's going on, Lieutenant?"

"There's been a shooting in Baton Rouge." He had no way of knowing that I had already gotten word about the shooting or that I was already in Baton Rouge.

He continued, "I need you to get over there and secure the area and to remain on alert just in case things take a turn for the worse. The kind of crowds that gather at times like this always make the situation worse."

"Was the shooting bad?" I inquired.

"What the hell does that matter? I need you to get your ass over there and make sure we take care of our own."

His response could not have been less endearing or more in alignment with the devilish truth that had been confirmed so many times before. In his mind and in the mind of so many who upheld the laurels of systemic racism, Black lives didn't matter. The lieutenant's failure to answer the question presented directly also let me know that the officer really fucked up. And his eagerness to hang up the phone sealed the deal. Personally conflicted and in preparation to follow professional orders, I glanced at the back seat of the car and noticed that I had a spare uniform, which meant that I wouldn't even have to drive back home to get dressed.

No sooner than the call with the lieutenant ended, a text from Derrick's came through. It was obvious that he too was now aware of the shooting.

"It's bad," I replied. He responded immediately. "Meet us there, we're all on our way."

I took a deep breath in through my nose and blew the steam of frustration out through my mouth. En route to the shooting scene, I felt like Dr. Jeckyll and Mr. Hyde amidst an internal battle back and forth with myself about whether or not to put on my uniform and join my fellow officers or to remain in my street clothes and join my fellow revolutionaries. In the moment, justice for all was questionable at best.

When I arrived at Mckinley Street, where the shooting had occurred, I observed a large crowd of citizens yelling at police officers and holding up signs. I made the decision to get dressed in uniform in the car. I could hear the voices of the people, and it was obvious that the devil was in the details as tempers flared and emotions ran high. The screams of the civilians revealed the exhaustion of a people pleading to a crowd of officers, many of whom lacked grace or mercy for those who had been oppressed and traumatized by the state of the country and years of unacknowledged oppression and pain. The officers, my counterparts, were laser focused on protecting the first responders rendering aid to the lifeless body of the young Black male on the ground. The expectation in uniform was that I would do the same. Had I not seen this scenario countless times before, I might have been moved to tears, but the unfortunate truth of desensitization was all too real. All I wanted to do was to make it better for those who hurt, but I was torn on the best way to do so. Plagued by thoughts and confirmations of the fact that inaction also meant injustice, I was thrust into movement.

While standing in the middle of the street alone, fully dressed in my uniform, I could feel the presence of three more bodies standing behind me. Derrick, Meisha, Joshua, made me feel as if I stood on the shoulders of giants. And before I knew it, I would be forced to make good on my promises to choose a side. In the distance, I could see Kevin and the rest of the group standing behind the angry crowd of civilians.

"I'm not sure what is happening here, but all I know is that I can't continue to allow it to happen on my watch. The people deserve better than this. We deserve better than this." My words were laced with fire and free from fear of what could be.

"Y'all do know that if I am caught out here doing anything other than aligning with blue that I will be fired."

"Fuck that bro. As of today, you're aligned with Black," Derrick confirmed.

In my heart, I knew he was right. I'd made my decision long ago, but today was a day of reckoning. From my peripheral, I could see the angry crowd advancing toward the officers and first responders. I also noticed the civilians growing in number and knew that it would not be long before they outnumbered the officers. It was now or never. "We can't let this happen, let's get in formation." My words to Meisha, Derrick, and Joshua were final.

"Well, you in charge, call it out," Derrick responded.

Without hesitation, I yelled to my group "ATTENTION!!"

I could see the 80-plus members now present snap to attention just as we'd practiced. The civilians and officers turned to take notice. They were staring in confusion. Outside of the military, they had never seen anything like us. Our uniformity commanded attention.

"Forward march!!"

I was now leading my group toward the crowd. They miraculously parted, allowing us to march through. The open space gave way to my lieutenant, who was standing in front of the group of officers. His face was riddled with disgust and confusion from my actions. Instead of shouting expletives, he stood in silence as his face turned beet red.

By the time I reached him, I raised my right fist, signaling for the group to stop behind me. When the group came to a halt, I stood face to face with my lieutenant.

"What the fuck are you doing with all of this?!! This is a shit show you're creating here," he exclaimed.

"I'm doing what all of us commissioned to help people should be doing. Protecting & Serving, sir!!"

The lieutenant began again, "Your ass…"

I cut him off from speaking. Standing before him and the army that I now led, I pulled my badge from my pocket and slapped it into his hand. "Never again will I stand behind one of our own just because they're our own. I no longer stand behind your fucked-up definition of protecting & serving. As a matter of fact, you need to reevaluate that shit!!" I leaned in closer and said, "Now I'm about to turn around and walk out of here with the soldiers that I've assembled. If you were smart, y'all would take this chance to get the hell out of here too."

I turned to face my group who were still standing at attention and lifted my right fist in the air before the next command.

"ABOUT!!! FACE!!!!" The group swiftly turned in the opposite direction. "FORWARD MARCH!!" We all marched back through the open crowd in the same synchronous manner in which we had entered. The lieutenant and the other officers wisely followed behind me as the first responders loaded the body of the young man into the ambulance and drove out behind us. We continued to march until the ambulance was clear of the large crowd of civilians.

The lieutenant and his officers quickly got into their vehicles and left the scene.

Before dispersing, I assured the group that I would be fine after the encounter. In my heart and in my soul, I knew that it was important to let them see that we possess just as much power and influence as law enforcement does when organized and operating in purpose. For me, the fight against injustice was purposeful enough.

CHAPTER TEN

THE HIGH PRIEST

GIVE ME LIBERTY OR GIVE ME DEATH.

The next morning when I awoke, the lines between my dreams and reality were somewhat blurred. I'd be lying if I said that my emotions weren't mixed because they were. I was well aware that my choice between black and blue came with a price, but so did my soul, and I had deemed before everyone at the protest that it wasn't for sale.

Derrick arranged a meeting with me, Meisha and Joshua. When I arrived, we exchanged dap and sat down, immediately getting to work. Joshua spoke first.

"I've been working with Derrick to convince my grandpa, who is a priest, to allow a few members of the group to come and speak at the church."

"And what did he say," I inquired.

"He was extremely reluctant, but he finally agreed. The service takes place later on tonight and it would be a perfect time to have our voices be heard. The congregation is composed mostly of politicians, business owners and folks with influence."

"It's an opportunity that we can't afford to miss," Derrick chimed in.

I nodded in agreement and noticed that Meisha was uncharacteristically quiet. Instead of speaking her mind like normal, she just stared at the ground as if she was in a trance.

"Are you okay," I asked. She nodded and reassured me that she was fine, before standing up and saying, "I'll catch up with yall later." Without explanation, she left. In agreement with the next move, we all stood and went our separate ways. I spent the rest of the day deep in thought and accepting the fact that things for me would never be the same. I justified my actions by acknowledging the fact that things had never been equal for me in the first place. No matter what side of the war I was on, I was still a member of the oppressed. Now, facing consequences and repercussions of my actions to denounce my role as an officer, I had to plot my next moves to ensure that my people prospered. I paced back and forth in my apartment, thinking that I would at least hear from the lieutenant to tell me directly that I was fired, but the call never came. And before I knew it, the time to attend the service arrived and I redirected my focus towards the events that were to take place.

When I arrived, my nerves attempted to get the best of me. Instead of entering the service, I forked off to the bathroom to gather myself. From there, I could hear the priest closing out his sermon over the speaker, which was an indicator that I didn't have much time left before I was to speak. After forcing myself to leave the restroom, I did everything possible to prevent my nerves from getting the best of me. Nearing the sanctuary, I noticed Derrick sitting in a chair outside of the door with his face buried in his hands, which let me know that he gave up on rushing me out of the restroom.

Now standing in his personal space, I tapped him on his shoulder. "Let's go cuz, I'm ready."

"Well it's about time, man. I never heard anybody talk to themselves as much as you did inside of that restroom. I didn't think you were ever coming out," Derrick said.

I smiled and hugged him as he stood up. "Let's get this over with."

We both walked out and took our seats just behind the priest, who was standing at the podium. Kevin and Joshua were both seated towards the front of the congregation. Joshua gave me a thumbs-up and Kevin nodded his head in confirmation. I looked for Meisha, but she was nowhere to be found. My sweaty palms served as a constant reminder of just how nervous I was. This was one of the largest Catholic churches in Baton Rouge and it was filled to capacity. I had previously learned that Joshua and his family were raised in this church. His father and granddad, who were ex-cops, founded the church. Continuing to gaze across the audience allowed me to check the pulse of the room. Joshua's granddad was not excited about allowing me to speak at his church, so it took Joshua some time to finally convince him to allow me to speak today. And Joshua's dad was nowhere to be found.

From the moment that Joshua told me just about every local judge, politician, both senators, congressman, and business owner either attended this church or were former members of this church, I knew this was our biggest chance at winning them over. This was our opportunity to speak to the people who had the most influence to create and amend laws. This room had the power to affect how law enforcement enforced the law. Our goal today was simple and had not changed from our previous protests. We desired to get the attention of the people who were seated that day. Once we had their attention, we needed them to understand the fury of systemic racism. We needed them to recognize that the Black and Brown people of America were catching hell in almost every sector of life with no justice in sight. Most importantly we needed them to understand that the same hell we were catching would soon become the hell they would experience if things didn't change.

The priest looked back at me with a look of uncertainty on his face before turning back to the microphone and saying, "Well family, we have a guest speaker here today. He's a young man who is a close friend of my grandson, so I would like for us to take a second before departing the Lord's house to hear what the young man has to say. Church family, let's welcome Elijah Steele into the house of the Lord."

I stood and adjusted my necktie as I made my way to the podium. My nerves worked overtime to get the best of me. With every step I took towards the podium, my feet felt as if they were weighed down by concrete blocks. I shook the priest's hand and smiled as best I could as he backed away and took his seat.

While waiting for the welcoming applause to quiet down, I looked around the church to see all of the curious White faces staring directly at me.

Clearing my throat before speaking, "Thank you all for allowing me to speak here today. I won't keep you long, but there are some things I need to say. Some things that are not only important to me and my loved ones, but to all of you and your loved ones as well. As I prepared my mind to come out here and speak to you today, I was set on giving you a brief lesson on Black history, American history, and reminding you of all of the pain Blacks have endured in America. I also had some fancy quotes from the beautiful Dr. Maya Angelou, but I won't spend too much time on things we already know. In light of the protest which took place earlier today, I'll start with a quote from the late great Reverend Dr. Martin Luther King Jr.:

I think America must see that riots do not develop out of thin air. Certain conditions continue to exist in our society which must be condemned as vigorously as we condemn riots. But in the final analysis, a riot is the language of the unheard. What is it that America has failed to hear? It has failed to hear that the plight of the Negro poor has worsened over the last few years. It has failed to hear that the promises of freedom and justice have not been met, and it has failed to hear that large segments of white society is more concerned about tranquility and status quo than about justice, equality and humanity. So in a real sense our nation's summers of riots are caused by our nation's winters of delay and as long as America postpones justice, we stand in the position of having these recurrences of violence and riots over and over again. Social justice and progress are the absolute guarantors of riot prevention.

"While I was seated behind the podium as the priest spoke, I had the chance to look around the congregation at all of the smiling faces.

Everyone in here from the youngest child to the older adults seemed to be carefree and completely happy to be in the Lord's house, as you all should be. No one seems concerned about whether there is someone amongst the congregation packing a pistol and waiting to unload his pistol on the innocent men, women and children here today."

The smiles on everyone's faces seemed to disappear instantly. Small chatter amongst the church members began to take place. I knew I had their attention now.

I continued on, "No one here is concerned whether there is a bomb planted inside the church that will explode and kill everyone you love. Congregations in Black churches don't have this liberty. In places like Carolina or Texas, they aren't feeling the same levels of comfort that you all felt prior to me speaking here today. The look of discomfort, concern and uncertainty that is on your faces right now is the exact look Blacks have on their faces when they are inside their churches. The fear that came over you when I mentioned someone possibly doing harm to you for no apparent reason is the fear Blacks face when they encounter a racist police officer. If I could get everyone, just for a minute, to close your eyes."

The chatter amongst the congregation began again and a few were shaking their heads in disagreement with my request. Everyone was uneasy and quickly losing interest in what I had to say.

Joshua had to have felt the same energy I felt. When we locked eyes, he nodded his head and stood to his feet. Kevin stood beside Joshua as they both closed their eyes. I looked back as the priest and Derrick stood in agreement. The priest, before closing his eyes, signaled to the entire church to rise to their feet.

After every member was standing with their eyes closed, I continued...

"With your eyes closed, imagine a race of people approximately four hundred years ago living on one of the world's most resourceful continents amongst their own kind, until one day, an evil race of people decided for no good reason they were going to kidnap the first race and transport them to a piece of land recently stolen by the evil race. For the next two hundred years the captured race would be stripped of their culture, language, spirituality and reduced to workers with no compensation. They would be sold amongst the evil race as cattle, hung from trees, beaten, raped, tortured, and worked to death. The captured race of people would endure this horrific treatment even after they were reluctantly 'set free.' They were set free on paper but continued to be treated like animals by the evil race. Despite the mistreatment and lack of humanity, for the next one hundred and fifty years the captured race never gave up hope of one day being totally free, mind, body and soul. They endeavoured to be free from mental and physical bondage, free to love themselves, and free to enjoy fruits of the free labor their ancestors were forced to give this country.

"I want you all to keep your eyes closed and try to get a good picture in your mind of the faces of that struggling race of people. Try to feel the pain and sorrow they felt over the last three hundred plus years. Imagine the unjust lynching. Imagine how the innocent children felt as they watched the bodies of their parents hanging from trees swaying from side to side as the wind blew.

"Can you feel that struggling race's pain? Can you imagine the hurt they had to feel on a daily basis knowing what they were up against?"

I peered out into the congregation to notice that some were nodding their heads in agreement with me.

"Now I need you to imagine that the people who were kidnapped from their land and stripped of everything they ever knew, imagine that they were White!"

Everyone, including Kevin and Joshua, opened their eyes. Joshua's facial expression went from shocked to a look of understanding and compassion. The church members began whispering amongst themselves again.

"Could you all imagine living in piss poor neighborhoods with the ones you love? Could you imagine those neighborhoods being policed by a majority of Black cops with renegade attitudes? Black cops who constantly targeted, beat and killed your loved ones. Imagine crying, begging and pleading for justice only for your cries to fall on deaf ears because the majority of all judges, lawmakers and attorneys were Black! What would you do?! How long would you be able to endure the unfair treatment and the killings of your loved ones on cell phone videos? What would you do? Protest until your arms are tired of holding signs? March until your feet are blistered and scream for justice until your lungs are sore? If you and your people did all of those peaceful things for hundreds of years in an attempt to achieve equality only to be ignored, what would you do?"

The church remained silent. Two White kids sitting on the front bench next to their mother caught my eye. They were both whispering to one another and sharing laughs as kids did. Then it hit me...

I focused my attention on the mother of the two kids. "Ma'am, how old are your two boys?" I asked as she looked around wondering if I was speaking to her. "Yes, you, ma'am. How old are your boys? Ten or twelve maybe?"

"Yes," she said as she quickly nodded her head.

"And your name, please?"

"Mary."

"You have two beautiful boys, Ms. Mary," I said with a smile as she smiled back. "I once learned of a mother just like you, Mary, who had a son around the age of your twelve-year-old boys. The mother lived in the northern part of the United States with her son. She decided one summer to send her son down south to Mississippi to visit with his cousins and other family members. One day the young boy and his cousins visited a nearby corner store that was run by a White female and her family. As the young boy and his cousins made their purchases in the store and walked out, the White store clerk walked out to her vehicle which was parked beside the store. As she walked to the vehicle, the young boy from up north supposedly whistled at the White store clerk before he and his cousins traveled back to their home nearby. Later that week at approximately two-thirty on a Sunday morning, two White men who were relatives of the store clerk entered the young boy's home armed with guns. When they found the young boy from up north sleeping in bed, the two men dragged him out of the home and took him away in a pickup truck. The young boy's body would be discovered in the Tallahatchie River three days later by fishermen. His head had been attached to a seventy-four pound cotton gin fan bound with barbed wire in an attempt to sink his body. After learning of her son's death and having to fight to have her son's remains transported back to their home state, the grieving mother made a decision to have an open casket funeral service. She wanted the world to see what the White men had done to her baby boy.

"Mary, can you imagine the pain the mother felt?" I asked as she lowered her head and the tears began rolling down her cheek. "Could you imagine having to see your little boy lying in a pine box with his body mangled beyond anything you've ever seen? How would it make you feel if his eyes were beaten out of his skull? His head cracked open with an axe. His little tongue cut from his mouth and a bullet hole through the side of his head!"

Without lifting her head, as she began to cry out loud, Mary grabbed her two sons and quickly walked to the rear of the congregation, where she exited the church.

The sniffling and soft whispering filled the church until I began speaking again.

"Fortunately for all of you, this is not your reality. You are not the race who has suffered and begged for equality for all of these years. It's me and my people who are feeling the continuous pressure of oppression. How long do you ignore the problem or offer little to no relief to the problem? As I look around the congregation today, I see lawyers, judges, business owners, and members of the community. Everyone here today has an opportunity to help shed light on the issues we face as a community of people. Will you choose to continue to stand by while equality is still an issue? Will you wait until the oppressed people of Louisiana and America bring the pain they are feeling to your front door or inside of your church where you're supposed to be at peace? Or will you use your position in life for the greater good? While most things can't and won't happen overnight, I believe that we should act immediately to change the things we can change. Allowing Black officers to patrol and supervise their own communities would represent a start in the right direction. Of course they would be expected to do their jobs, but I'm confident that the number of unjustified shootings would drastically decline. The more an officer and citizen have in common, the better the understanding, communication and compassion would be between the two.

"Imagine the outcome if compassion was inserted in Tamir Rice's situation. Imagine the outcome if compassion was inserted when Walter Scott turned his back to run away from that officer. Insert compassion into Sandra Bland's traffic stop, Alton Sterling's CD selling, Eric Garner's cigarette selling, Trayvon Martin's stroll with his hoodie on, or Philando Castille riding with his family. The list goes on, but I believe compassion would have caused a different outcome. Well, I pray you will make the right decision, and I pray we're able to overcome these problems for the sake of us all. God bless and thanks for your time."

I turned and shook the priest's hand before walking away from the pulpit. As he extended his hand to shake mine, the tattoo on his forearm caught my eye. It seemed familiar but I could not place where I had seen it before, and the robe fell back down covering his arm rather quickly, so I just continued out to the church doors. The congregation didn't make a sound. I could hear a few sniffles, which was enough for me. That meant what I had said reached someone, and I was satisfied with that.

As I made my way out of the doors of the church, I heard a voice in the distance, "Elijah, wait!" It was Derrick and the rest of the group. I guess I was so focused on getting out of the church, I forgot to say goodbye.

"Still no sign of Meisha, right?" I asked Derrick.

Derrick shrugged, "No, we haven't heard from her. But look man, what you did in there was dope. I think you found your new calling," he said sarcastically.

"Yeah, right," I replied.

"Josh, I guess we can't expect any favors from your grandpa again after what happened in there, right?"

Josh looked at me and took a deep breath, "He'll be okay. I'll talk to him. My dad is a little easier to talk to, too bad he couldn't be here. Look, man, I never told anyone this but ever since I was a little boy, my family has always done things for families that were less fortunate than us, no matter if they were Black, White or whatever. They would oftentimes donate food, clothes, and even money to whomever was in need, but it was always done anonymously. My guess is that my family was afraid of the backlash they would have received from their peers for helping Blacks. My family and our church needed this today, Elijah. No matter the outcome from this, you have altered the mindset of this church, so thank you, brotha."

I held his words in high esteem. It was at that moment that I confirmed what I had always known. On that day, standing in front of a crowd of people who looked nothing like me, I recognized that I was far more powerful than I had ever given myself credit for being. I was standing on the shoulders of my ancestors and there was enough power to be the change I desired to see in the world inside my DNA.

CHAPTER ELEVEN

DEAFENING SILENCE

BE IT RESOLVED THAT THOSE WHO PLAY WITH FIRE,
WILLINGLY ELECT SMOKE IN THEIR EYES.

The next day, I made up my mind that I was going to locate Meisha myself. Sitting in my living room with the T.V. watching me, I realized that I was concerned about her for one reason or another. My mind wandered towards the notion that she was not well or that she might have gotten cold feet about working together after all that transpired between us. And even if I hadn't said it to anyone, I had grown accustomed to having her present for moral support. Truth be told, she was the power and the force behind the movement that we were building together. And although Derrick was my cousin, I now saw both Meisha and Joshua as family too. My first attempt was picking up the phone to call her, to no avail. My second attempt was throwing on some clothes and making a trip out to her house. I had the day all to myself and considered it to be a blessing as I still had heard nothing from the lieutenant. In my case, no news was good news after everything that transpired at the protest. No sooner than I placed the phone down to walk towards my bedroom, I got sidetracked by the flashing lights on the T.V. screen. The headline read, man 65, strangled in home. After working on the force for so many years, I was somewhat desensitized to the news. I knew that sooner or later I would find out the details through my own network. No sooner than I began to walk towards the bedroom to get dressed, I heard my phone vibrate, so I turned around to retrieve it and read the message while getting ready. After noticing that it was from Derrick, I resolved to call him back after I got dressed. I was certain that he wanted to recap the speech at Joshua's grandfather's church. Before I could reply, Derrick was already sending a text through. It read:

Did you hear about Joshua?

My mind began racing. Had someone hurt Joshua in retaliation for our protest? I immediately called Derrick back. By the time he picked up the phone he was out of breath. "What's going on bro? Is everything okay?

"Man, we need to get over to Joshua's house asap. It's a 911 emergency. He found his dad dead this morning. Someone strangled him in his office last night."

"Say no more, I'm on my way."

I threw my clothes on in haste and got moving.

By the time I placed my shirt over my head, I had connected the dots that the news story was about Joshua's dad. It made sense that the news coverage was paramount considering he was a retired cop. And by the time I got into the car, news of Joshua's father's death began spreading like wildfire. Reporters were sharing the story on almost every local radio channel and the alerts on my phone were going crazy. My mind raced as I tried to make sense of it all.

While stopped at a red light, I was startled by an alert from Christine at the crime lab referencing the evidence I submitted. It read:

"Here you go. Please never mention this to anyone." DNA from the clothing Meisha's mother was wearing during her struggle with the officers inside her boutique shop matched Joshua's dad.

I was so shocked, I could hardly drive. The horn from the car behind me was my reminder that I was even driving. How in the hell was Joshua's dad's DNA on the clothing worn by Meisha's mother? Immediately my mind began assembling the pieces of the jigsaw puzzle.

What I knew for sure was that Josh needed us and I was doing everything in my power legally to get there. By the time I arrived, I noticed

Derrick's car parked across the street. He knew better than to attempt to go inside based on the havoc we had been wreaking in the streets in the name of justice. Me on the other hand, I was technically still a member of law enforcement as I had not been formally terminated. And since I knew some of the officers surrounding the house in an effort to secure the crime scene, I gained entry.

Once inside, I could hear a familiar voice, and as I got closer, I could tell that it was Josh. He was in his father's office, the exact room where his father's body had been prior to being removed by the coroner. He was in the corner just behind the desk beside himself and rightfully so.

When we made eye contact, I could tell that he was in distress. He looked up at me and said, "None of this shit makes sense bro. Who would have done something like this? All I've ever done is fight to help other people and this is the thanks I get?"

Unsure of what to say amidst a tumultuous moment of loss and sorrow, I knelt down beside him with my back against the wall.

"So you have no idea who would have done something like this bro? Is there anyone who would have attempted retaliation of any kind?

He nodded his head in sorrow before responding. "Not that I can think of."

I noticed next to his hands, a small video tape and a sheet of paper. Joshua began to bang his hands against both sides of his head. The tears streamed down his face profusely as he began to rock back and forth. He was beside himself. The rage of the moment was inescapable and I was left to help Josh pickup the pieces. Unfortunately I knew his pain, it was the same pain I had spoken about in his grandfather's church the night before.

And although Joshua could hardly speak, he mustered up the strength to utter words that would stay with me for the rest of my life.

"No justice, no peace."

We had chanted those words in the streets together amidst protest, but never before had the phrase rang so clearly.

Still attempting to make sense of it all, I motioned for the note that was beside Joshua awaiting his permission to read it. He closed his eyes and handed it to me.

The note read:

These are the remnants of what appears to be a never ending war waged on us.

If I could take all of this back, I wouldn't.

There has been no justice served for me, only loss.

My only way out was through.

This video should give you the rest of the answers that you need.

Josh held the video tightly in his hands. I didn't need to watch it to know what was on it. With the confirmation of the DNA placement from Christine, I had enough information to draw my own conclusions.

The death of Josh's father was the dissarest that I had warned the congregation of the church about. Scores of generations have been held down with necks pressed into the pavement of injustice in search of equality. The lack thereof has established thoughts of mutiny. As long as we lived in a country that allowed and encouraged peaceful protests to fall upon deaf ears, war would become a means to an end. Now we must ask ourselves if in the end we desire to have famine that comes from war, or prosperity that comes from peace?

I began reminiscing back to the night Meisha and I spent together and the conversation we had…

There was no way I could have forgotten the look on Meisha's face when she asked me, "When does our pain go away or will it ever go away?"

My response to her that night was jarring.

"I guess sometimes when you've exhausted all other reasonable means, the only thing left to do is pinpoint that thing that pains you the most and eliminate it from your life the best way you know how."

Still sitting beside Joshua, I couldn't help but to wonder if this was Meisha's way of eliminating her pain?

What I knew for sure in the moment as I helped Joshua to his feet was that pain was paralyzing. Joshua would be forced to live the rest of his life with the same hole in his heart that Meisha had carried around for so many years. When war is waged, there are no victors, only casualties.

LOVE AND REVOLUTION

Two months had passed since the morning that Joshua discovered his father and alot changed. Joshua was attempting to put the pieces of his life back together and rightfully so. Derrick continued on the mission to fight injustice and to immobilize people for the greater good. Not only had I not personally heard from Meisha, but her face was now all over the news. She was wanted for questioning in reference to the murder of Joshua's dad. Some people in the city, and particularly the Black community, were referring to the incident as poetic justice after learning that Meisha's mother had been attacked and sexually assaulted by Joshua's father and grandfather before senselessly losing her life, amidst a tragedy such as Hurricane Katrina. The news also gained wind of the fact that Meisha was at Joshua's dad's home that night in search of answers and clues about how her mother died. She had always been out for justice, but never with intent to harm or kill anyone, until her own life was in jeopardy. Meisha assumed that Joshua's dad would be at the service with everyone else and deemed it safe to search Joshua's dad's home. When Joshua's dad arrived back ahead of schedule, he caught her in his home and attempted to rape and kill her much like what had been done to her mother. It was reported that she was in a fight for her life, and left the note in angst and consideration of a justice system that she knew would fail her. Her fight for her life was one in which she won.

I had been placed on administrative leave from the force and was utilizing each day to strategize my transition into law school. I recognized more than ever that the battle for injustice can be fought from many different positions.

One day, after checking the mail in hopes of receiving my confirmation of sitting for the LSAT, I received an anonymous letter with no return address. By the time I got back to the door of my apartment, I had already consumed half of its contents and I knew without question that it was from Meisha.

It read:

In case you were wondering, she's in Cuba. She has managed to discover peace through the pain. She knows a beautiful young lady who works at a coffee shop in Santa Clara. She oftens speaks of falling in love with a man before being forced to move far away. One day, she hopes to see him again. She desires to tell him that he planted a seed of love the night they were together.

Gasping for air, I was forced to use the wall near the doorway of my apartment to hold me up. Every attempt to hold back my tears failed. Never in a million years had I imagined that the night I shared with Meisha would result in the creation of life. My desire to be with her was greater than ever, but we couldn't. Me locating her would not only place her in trouble, but also compromise the baby that we had created together. Somehow the video of her mom's encounter with the officer had also made its way to the mass media, confirming the fact that Joshua's father and grandfather had been responsible for her mother's demise. Joshua's granddad had been arrested and their family left to mourn the loss of not one but two of its anchors, who had proven themselves morally corrupt. It was an unfortunate series of events for Joshua to endure, especially after all he attempted to fight in the face of injustice. And now, injustice was knocking at his front door.

By the time I could catch my breath long enough to get back inside I attempted to get over the initial shock of the information shared in the letter. I sat on the couch for at least 20 minutes in shock before attempting to write a response and eventually made my way to the kitchen table with a pen and a few pieces of paper and two envelopes.

"To My Assata"

There is a lost love in search of the touch and feel of a love he once knew, one he had dreams of calling his own. The abrupt loss of her presence taught him that nothing is promised, and further proves that we must learn to savor moments of joy.

It is in the sentiment of new life that he finds himself honored to be deemed a creator. Birth signifies new beginnings.

Because of her will to fight, local politicians have begun to make changes. There are more Black officers patrolling Black neighborhoods, real Black history is being taught in the schools and the BUY BLACK & BUY BACK slogan has gone from a hashtag to a full blown movement. The local celebrities have even chipped in. And as you read this letter, businesses, property and land are being purchased.

As for her lover, he's still protecting and serving, in a different kind of uniform. He dreams of the day that he can meet his new family.

Tears streamed down my face as I wrote each word because I knew without question that her fight had not been in vain. I addressed each of the envelopes to the only two coffee shops I could locate in Santa Clara. In very small letters across the bottom right corner of each envelope, I wrote, "Know justice, know peace." For me, until that day, justice and peace were two prolific sentiments that had been withheld from me until that day. The true soldier fights not because he despises what is in front of him, but because he desires to love and to protect what is in front of him.

OUTRO

A BIRD'S EYE VIEW

THE RIGHT PERSPECTIVE HAS THE POWER
TO MAKE THE UNJUST JUST.

As a child you're not born with a background in psychiatry, so in many instances, trauma also lends a lack of understanding. For that reason alone, I didn't understand that being molested as a child possibly contributed to my acting out later in life. I didn't understand that not having my parents around made me behave a certain way. I didn't understand that watching my parents smoke crack in front of me, being exposed to sex, death, and violence could alter the way I perceived the world.

That altered perception made me who I am today as a man and officer. We all understand that when we were young kids, we hadn't begun to value good decision-making or how it could affect us in the future. At least not until we were old enough to distinguish between what's right and what's wrong. For that reason I don't regret my past because most of it I had no control over. I have learned to appreciate my past, especially now in my line of work. The power to take someone's freedom lies within the stroke of my pen and the power to take that person's life lies within the retraction of my trigger finger. Despite that, my power to love and sympathize with people, no matter their skin color, sexual orientation, class, or race always repelled any thought of misusing the power of my pen or actions of my trigger finger. I couldn't speak the same for my co-workers and wasn't too sure they were in a position to speak the same of themselves.

For we all come from different walks of life, therefore our perception of life is different. Someone may argue that the last statement is an excuse to misuse power. To be clear, that is a statement of fact which points to only one of the few reasons the outcome of someone's encounter with an officer may be positive or negative. For instance, if I am a White officer who was raised around hatred for Blacks and people of a different race, depending on if I decided to embrace my past or reject it will have a major influence on how my encounters with Black citizens play out.

I apply the same line of thinking for myself as a Black officer. If I allowed the environment I grew up in to dictate the way I thought today, I would walk around with the notion that every White officer was bad and every White person was out to get me. Fortunately I am able to think for myself and judge people individually so that I am able to provide myself with a realistic outlook of the society in which I live.

On paper, officers are expected to treat everyone fairly and with respect no matter the person's race. Realistically or even logically, this can't be expected of a young officer who hasn't yet learned how to be a man before becoming an officer, nor can it be expected of an officer who was raised on the basis of hate or disdain for another race. When considering those factors, this expectation of fairness is psychologically unlikely to occur. What we decide to do about this truth and how we take action to address the plight for justice in the face of injustice is up to us.

Unarmed Black people losing their lives at the hands of White officers who operate from the bowels of systemic racism is never acceptable and therefore calls for revolution and dismantling of the systems that plague our existence. There can be no peace in the absence of justice.

AUTHOR BIO

Elijah Steele is a father, longstanding officer, investor, author, and future attorney from the Westbank of New Orleans. Elijah has used each moment of life to manifest his destiny amidst and triumph against all odds. As a self-described servant of the people, he finds gratitude in working to ensure the prosperity of marginalized people.

CONNECT WITH THE AUTHOR
ON SOCIAL MEDIA

WEBSITE: WWW.NWBBOOK.COM

INSTAGRAM: @ELIJAH__STEEL

FACEBOOK: ELIJAH STEELE

EMAIL: NWBBOOKI@GMAIL.COM

CPSIA information can be obtained
at www.ICGtesting.com
Printed in the USA
BVHW031501080822
644064BV00015B/474

9 781953 156341